MY
HEART

MY

HEART

MELANIE VEARES

For Luke, forever in my heart

x x x

'Love is from the infinite and will remain until eternity.'

RUMI

Chapter 1

The Beginning of the End

A s the early morning sun streamed into the room through the brightly coloured cotton curtains, Grace Sullivan slowly started to come to and open her eyes. She took a moment to take in her surroundings, until the familiarity of the primrose floral wallpaper and her various ornaments and pictures began to awaken her senses. She lay there for a moment staring at the particles of dust, dancing around in the sunshine; admiring the beauty of the dance with its twisting and turning motions moving to the rhythm of the breeze blowing in through the open window; envying the freedom of just being able to bob around doing your own thing without a care in the world. She smiled inwardly to herself at the irony of it. A few years ago, she would have winced in horror at the dust and would have got her duster out and given the place a damn good clean. Now here she was lying in bed in her final days admiring the beauty of it.

At first, when she was woken by the bright light blinding her eyes, she wondered whether she had died and gone to heaven in the night. She was quite disappointed when she realised that she hadn't. For a while now she knew that she was in her final days; she had been visited by her mother and her son, both in spirit. They had stood at the end of her bed, a vision of perfect health with a beautiful glow of light surrounding them. They didn't speak, they just smiled at her and at one point her son reached out his arms towards her. It was such a long time since she had last seen him, many, many years ago and yet it felt like yesterday when she saw him. Her heart melted and leapt at the thought of being reunited with him once again.

She had officially been diagnosed with a failing heart, but she knew there was nothing wrong with her heart. She was just tired of living; it was time to go home. She was excited and yet sad at the same time. She desperately missed her husband who had died a couple of years ago and couldn't wait to see her loved ones, especially her son. But she would miss her oldest son and his beautiful wife and her gorgeous brood of grandchildren and great-grandchildren. Her bones were weary though. She was fed up with feeling weak all the time and not being able to do all the things she had used to do. Up until recently she had been living independently, doing her own shopping, housework and even gardening. But then she had that stupid fall, and that put paid to that. If only she had been more careful! But there was no point in dwelling on it. She hadn't been careful and that was that. She'd been laid up for weeks with a broken leg and that's when things started to go downhill. The last thing she wanted was to be a burden to her family. So, for the last six weeks, there she was at 86 years old, staying in Cherry Tree nursing home waiting to die.

Oh, they were nice enough here, she thought; the room was pleasant and the staff were friendly. But she missed her little bungalow and garden, and being able to sit outside watching all her flowers and shrubs starting to bloom, for it was late spring and she knew her garden would be a feast for the eyes. She loved sitting outside with her morning cup of tea listening to the bees buzzing around and watching the birds washing themselves in the bird bath and pecking at all the little treats she used to leave out for them. She had an extremely tame blackbird that would often come and sit close to her, and start singing at the top of its voice with its glorious bird song. She thought that blackbirds had a beautiful song which could match any nightingale. She made a mental note to get the nurse to open the window wider so she could hear more of the birds. Her bed was too far from the window to see out which was such a shame, as the gardens were beautiful here, but they were very difficult to get to with all the steps. As she was too weak now to go outside, it would have been nice to look out the window. The rooms weren't very well laid out here. They maybe should have given a bit more thought to the people who were bedbound and what sort of view they would have.

She sighed wearily and turned towards the door as she heard Gina, the morning nurse, coming in to see her.

'Morning Grace,' she sung in her beautiful Irish accent. 'How are you this fine sunny morning, did you sleep well?' she said carrying in a tray with a plastic beaker of tea and some bowl of insipid-looking liquid. Gina was a short, rather rotund lady with thick dark wavy hair and beautiful blue eyes. Her complexion was pale but healthy looking and she had a lovely energy about her. Nursing was the perfect job for her, reflected Grace; she had the knack of lifting your spirits when she entered the room. 'Let's sit you up a bit and give you a nice cup of morning tea. My mammy always said you can't face the day until you've had your first taste of tea.' She pressed the button to raise the head of the bed so Grace was almost sitting up.

'Quite right too,' whispered Grace in between shallow breaths. 'I slept well thank you.' She tried to move her head forward as Gina brought the plastic beaker to her lips to drink. She swallowed a few mouthfuls and tasted the flavour of tea and plastic on her tongue. Yuck, she thought, reduced to sipping tea out of a toddler's beaker and even then, she didn't have the energy to hold the cup. Never mind, it won't be for much longer.

'Your son's coming to visit today. He phoned me this morning to check how you were.' She paused to take a look at Grace's face. 'I thought that would put a smile on your face,' she said as she started to feed Grace the foul-looking liquid. She was right though, that did put a smile on Grace's face. She loved her son with a passion. Both her sons were her pride and joy, her greatest achievement in life. She had always wanted sons and was thrilled when both her sons were born two years apart. They were good boys, hard work mind as they were always on the bounce the minute they opened their eyes, but they were kind and caring and never really gave her or her husband any bother. Grace and John, her husband, were devastated when they lost their youngest son, Michael. He died at 20 years old, way too young and under such terrible circumstances too. James, their oldest son, was traumatised for years following the death of his brother. They were best friends, so close. It took him a long time to get over his death, if he ever really did.

She pondered over her memories for a while, having flashbacks of times gone by. Then continued to take some more mouthfuls of the bland-tasting baby food. She was lifted however at the thought of her son's visit. She always enjoyed spending time in his company. He was such a personable man, everyone always loved him. Over the years it always amused Grace how James would start working for different companies and immediately have older women seeking his advice on relationships and dilemmas. They used to say how he was such a good listener and so easy to talk to. He was also tall, dark and extremely handsome so that may also have had something to do with it, she chuckled to herself. But, she reflected, he should have been a counsellor and maybe he would have been, but after his brother's death she wondered whether he just needed to have a time of peace and stability. He didn't have the energy to take on anyone else's baggage; it was hard enough for him to make sense of his own. So, career wise, he probably didn't go down the path that would have suited him fully – but who could blame him. He was badly wounded and probably needed something that didn't drain him emotionally. Mind you, he had done very well for himself from a financial aspect but Grace often felt he wasn't very fulfilled with his work and something more person-centred would have given him more job satisfaction.

He was also the reason that she and John hadn't gone completely insane after Michael's death. It kept them going, having to focus on James, making sure he was OK. They were both so proud of the man James had become, in spite of all the grief he had endured over the years. He was a good man, good husband and a good father. She used to burst with pride when she saw how gentle and tender he was with his children and grandchildren. She could have watched him all day. More recently, she had got into the habit of replaying in her mind scenes of James from years gone by, just like a movie. He was so caring and kind, she often used to say that he was an old soul. Sometimes she was astounded at the wisdom that came out of his mouth. But then Michael was the same. He was a very deep thinker and would often leave people speechless with some of the wise things he would say. One of his schoolteachers made a comment at his parents' evening to the effect she wasn't sure who was the teacher and who was the pupil. Grace felt blessed to have such wonderful memories to dwell on. She had lived such a long and full life, and was lucky to have had such happy times to look back on. The harder times she had buried in the depths of her core and built a steel box around it to boot, keeping them locked away tightly. It was very rare that they ever came out. She always felt that after Michael's death she was broken, that somehow she had fragmented into different pieces. A piece of her had died with Michael, never to be seen again. Another part of her was locked in that steel box; a toxic mixture of fury, rage, longing and desire; a torturous pain so overwhelming that she felt terrified of what would happen if it ever escaped. People thought that she was brave with how she had carried on after Michael's death, but she wasn't brave at all; she was a coward, too scared to acknowledge her feelings and emotions in case they consumed her and she was driven mad with grief. No. She had been better off locking that part of herself away and showing another fragmented part of herself that fooled the world and herself into believing that she could cope and looked in control of things. Her grief was still as raw as the day Michael died. She had just learned to live with it. The heaviness in her heart that was so painful at first was now a comfort to her. She felt as if she was carrying Michael around in her heart. For every Christmas, birthday or family celebration, Michael was where he should be, in amongst the heart of his family, safely tucked away enjoying the celebrations with them.

But after seeing Michael at the end of her bed looking so young and happy recently, she had a feeling that the lid was about to come off that steel box. In the beginning her loss was so immense and overwhelming that sometimes she felt she couldn't breathe. Her pain at the loss of what could have been was so severe that she had no choice but to bury it. She thought of the amount of herself that she had invested in her children from the day they were born. She only realised that, once the investment had been cut off and there was nowhere to send it any more. It had been a double-edged sword for Grace over the years, watching James marry and have children and move on in life, because for every bit of happiness James had, she mourned the loss of what should have been for Michael. She missed the excitement of daydreaming about Michael's future – wondering who he would marry, what type of career he would have, what would his children look like – which was ridiculous as he may have decided not to have had children. She was surprised at the strength of loss she felt over her lost, unborn, grandchildren. Michael had such a lovely girlfriend when he died. She remembered watching them snuggled on the sofa together watching films; how it used to give her such a warm, fuzzy feeling, thinking of how wonderful their future together could be. His girlfriend was heartbroken at Michael's death and it took her many years to recover; another thing that Grace had

had to grieve over. He also had some wonderful friends who loved him dearly and were devastated when he died too. It was incredible the number of losses that came flying at you from all different directions following a loved-one's death; it really was like throwing a stone in a pond and feeling the effect of the ripples reaching out far and wide. She shuddered and returned to happier thoughts and the upcoming visit of her son.

After she finished her breakfast and been given a wash-down in the bed, she was surprised to see James walking through the door. She wasn't expecting him so soon.

'Hello Mum, how are you doing?' he said, leaning over to kiss her. 'I hope you haven't been having those late-night parties and causing mayhem,' he joked. Her eyes softened as she looked admiringly at him, taking in his presence as he came into the room.

Grace smiled. 'I wish!' she whispered, chuckling. 'I'm fine. How are you darling?' she said, taking his hand.

'Yeah, I'm good thanks,' he said as he pulled the chair up next to her. 'Amanda sends her love. She'll be visiting at the weekend and the girls send their love too. Jess phoned last night, had a bit of a catch up with her.' He paused and adjusted himself in the seat before continuing. 'Richard's fine and JJ has started his apprenticeship course which he's enjoying. And I spoke to Mollie a couple of days ago. They're all OK. Jack is still working long hours and the twins are studying hard for their final exams at school, so

Mollie said the household was like a ticking time bomb! But apart from that, all's well,' he blurted out, clutching her hand with his other hand and giving it a bit of a squeeze. Grace could tell he was uptight as his voice was slightly too high and his words were being fired out quickly.

'That's good, I'm glad everyone is doing OK,' she smiled at him adoringly. James still had a thick crop of hair, although it was greying now, flecked with salt and pepper. She had always loved the way his fringe flopped over to the side and she looked at him fondly as she started to speak.

'Now I need to talk to you about something,' she paused and took a couple of breaths, struggling to get the words out. She knew she had to get to the point quickly, as she got so exhausted when she spoke and was worried she would tire before she said everything she wanted to. 'I know you don't like talking about it but you know my time here is running out.' James went to protest but she put her hand up. 'No! Don't start. I don't mind. I'm going to be going home. You know my beliefs. I've had a good life but I need to go home now. I need to see your father. I miss him. I also need to see Michael.' She faltered slightly. 'It's been such a long time. I need to see him again.' She stopped and caught her breath then whispered, 'But I promise you I'll be waiting for you when your time comes and I'll also send a little message to you so that you know I'm OK.' She squeezed his hand again and smiled; her eyes were now glassy from unshed tears.

James looked down at his mother, staring at her beautiful kind face. He loved this lady. She had always been his rock; the person he trusted more than anyone in the world. She had helped him through the darkest of days, even though he knew she was suffering terribly too. He couldn't imagine not having her in his life. At that moment he felt like a young boy needing his mother to be there to keep him safe. His heart started to thump and he felt anxiety start to creep into his body. 'Don't talk like that Mum, you'll be fine, you've got a few years left in you yet,' he declared unconvincingly.

'Now stop it, you know that's not true!' She stared at him and looked deeply into his eyes. 'You'll be OK, you're stronger than you think, and it's your turn to be the strong one for your beautiful family. But I promise you I'll send you a sign so you know I'm OK.' She started to tire now and took a moment to gather herself.

'Oh yeah,' smiled James. 'And how are you going to do that?' he said, gently mocking her.

'I shall send a robin to let you know I'm OK and waiting for you,' she whispered, tapping her nose and smiling. She truly believed that robins and white feathers were a sign from a loved one that had died, to let their loved ones know that all was OK in heaven.

James stroked her hand but didn't speak. He couldn't. He was far too choked. He knew the words wouldn't come but the unshed tears would. He remembered back to when his mother had called him in the early hours of the morning, to tell him Michael had died; how he had clung to her in sheer raw grief at the loss of his beloved brother. His brother Michael had always been his best friend. He had so many childhood memories of him and Michael, playing games together, out in the garden playing football; talking late into the night about different things, whether it be girls, football, school, all manner of things. They shared a room together and got on really well; they also seemed to like the same things. He knew that Michael adored him as he was the older brother and he followed him everywhere. But James didn't mind; he liked his company. He knew Michael was a very deep thinker, always had been. He also tended to have a glass half-empty type of attitude, which if he was allowed to wallow in things, could get him down. But when they were younger James was always there to pick him up and give him a bit of a lift.

Things started to get tough for Michael when he reached eighteen and had to start living in the adult world. The bottom line was, Michael didn't like the world very much; didn't feel as though he belonged there. He longed for something else. He couldn't see that a life of working, getting married, having children was what he wanted to do. Things just seemed to go downhill for him, then he couldn't see a way out. James was living away at the time with Amanda, in London. It was James's first time living away since uni and he had just landed his first job. He had been in London for about a year, when Michael decided one cold Sunday night in March to take his own life and end it all. The guilt that James felt was overwhelming. He knew deep down that it wasn't his fault but he kept thinking if he'd had more time to visit him or rung him more often, then he could have helped Michael like he used to when they were little. His parents had been wonderful, even though they were dying inside too, they still managed to make time for him and make sure James was their priority. Mum was such a strong woman. He often wondered how she coped, and she never seemed to break down and cry or show any emotions. Some might say that this suggested someone who was lacking in emotions or was deeply damaged, but it wasn't like that; she always knew what to say and when to say it. There was always feeling there, but somehow she managed to contain it. She told him once her grief was private between her and Michael, and that she kept her grief controlled to when she was ready to cry. He knew she had her faith. She wasn't religious but was very spiritual and would often say Michael had visited her in her dreams or meditations. Dad was strong too. Sometimes James thought he was the strongest one of any of us because he was Mum's rock and Mum was James's rock, so maybe he was carrying us all.

James also thought of Amanda and what a fantastic wife she was, supporting him through everything. In the early days, he must have been hell to live with. He made a mental note to tell her this and make more of an effort to show her how much he loved her. It was easy to take things for granted when you had been married as long as they had.

He watched as his mum started to doze off. He could see her fighting to keep awake but the effort of all that emotion and talking had wiped her out. He sat staring at her deep in thought. Mum was the last of his immediate family; soon when she was gone he would be an orphan, all on his own. Even though he was 61 years old it made him feel abandoned and scared. He knew in his heart of hearts he would be fine, but at this very moment, looking down on her he didn't feel strong; he felt incredibly vulnerable; he almost felt like shaking her and begging her to stay alive and not to leave him. He sat and pondered what would happen to her when she died. Mum was always telling him her take on it, but he couldn't quite allow himself to believe it. He trusted his mum and her opinions counted for a lot, but he was also quite a scientific person and liked to have proof about things. Everything spiritual was so airy-fairy; nothing was concrete or proven. He had had some really accurate readings from mediums over the years, but this still wasn't enough. Yes, they gave him a bit of a lift but why hadn't Michael shown himself to him in his dreams? If only he had some sort of sign, it would be easier to believe in life after death.

James spent most of the morning by his mother's side with her drifting in and out of sleep. When she finally awoke, she could see it was early evening, James had gone home and the room was just starting to get dark. The place seemed very quiet. Dinner must be over by now. She imagined everyone would be settling down to watch a bit of telly for the evening. There was a sitting room where the residents could sit, but most of them stayed in their rooms in the evening, watching television. She reflected on her time spent with James earlier, she was glad she had managed to talk to him about her death. She felt she could go now without any unfinished business. The financial side of things had been dealt with ages ago – everything was being left to James – but emotionally she needed to check that James understood exactly what was going to happen. She knew how ridiculous she must have sounded, for he was a grown man with his own family, but to her he was still her child, her responsibility. She would make sure that she would keep her promise and send a robin to him to let him know she was OK, but, more importantly, to help him to start believing that there was life after death. Sometimes she despaired of him. Over the years he'd had some wonderful readings from mediums, which Grace had organised for him. Whilst they did lift him a bit, it wasn't enough to convince him. She knew it wasn't personal enough. He would say maybe they'd found the information on social media, blah, blah, blah. She chuckled to herself; just wait James, I'll make sure you get a message that you can't ignore! She sighed, deeply content with her memories, and very slowly drifted back into a long, deep, sleep.

Chapter 2

Born into Heaven

It was exactly eleven minutes past one on the 1st May 2020 when Grace Sullivan took her last breath. After a sudden jolt, she found herself floating up very gently towards the ceiling. At first, she thought she was imagining it, but then she noticed that she had started to feel incredibly light. As light as a feather and she noticed that her bones weren't aching and her breathing wasn't laboured any more. The second thing she realised was she was able to see up towards the ceiling as well as down towards her body at the same time. She thought that was a most peculiar thing but also rather amazing too. It was then that she thought that she must be dead, that it's finally happened and this is it. She found herself starting to get quite excited, even though she had wished for this over the last few months. Now it was actually happening it was nothing like she'd imagined. But then how would it be? How could you possibly imagine the sensation of being out of your body and being able to see 360 degrees all around you at the same time? It was quite extraordinary. She was also relieved that it wasn't painful;

for, as much as she was ready to go, she was expecting a bit of pain or discomfort.

As she got used to the floating sensation, she started to move around the room. She looked down at her body lying there all tucked up under the blankets looking very pale and pathetic. She reminded herself of a waxwork model like the ones she had seen in Madam Tussauds. Funny, but she never really realised what she looked like until now. It's one thing looking in the mirror but another thing completely when you find yourself looking down on your body. How old and decrepit she had got! The years had not been kind to her, or was she just being vain? What was an 86-year-old supposed to look like anyway? In her mind, she was still in her thirties and quite a catch at that too. She was tall for a woman, about 5ft 8 inches. She was blessed with a slender body; well at least until she reached the menopause. She had kept her dark hair long, even though certain people used to take great delight in telling her how long hair aged you when you got over fifty. But she didn't care; she liked her hair long and only started to dye it when, in her fifties, she started to go grey. Her hairdresser would often remark how lucky she was that she hadn't gone grey any earlier as many people went grey in their thirties and forties or sometimes even earlier. But when she reached seventy, she decided to try and grow old a little bit more gracefully and she let her colour grow out. She remembered how her husband had told her every day how beautiful she was, right up until the day he died, and she had believed him too! Still, her body had served her well over the years; she had never had any real ailments over the whole of her life until the last few months. She was extremely fit and healthy, but she had worked hard to maintain her health over the years, eating healthily with lots of exercise, and for that she had reaped the rewards.

She was starting to enjoy the feeling of floating round the room. It made her feel carefree and liberated and reminded her of the particles of dust she had seen yesterday, dancing in the breeze. She wondered if she could float into another room, and with that thought headed straight into Joan's room next door. That's strange, she just thought of the room next door and, as if by magic, she was transported there. She took a second to get over the shock of it, as she felt quite disorientated with the speed that she'd moved. It was a little while before she looked down and noticed Joan lying in her bed. Poor love, she had an oxygen mask over her face and her short gasps were very laboured. Not long now and you too will be joining me Joan, she thought. She didn't really know her that well as most of the time they were kept in their rooms at the nursing home. But occasionally when they went down to the sitting room, if there was some music or entertainment going on, she would see her and they would often have a little chat. They had some local children come in at Easter to help them make Easter bonnets, which was very sweet. She had sat next to Joan then, although she looked a lot better then than she did now. Now she looked very frail and she'd lost a lot of weight too. She floated round the room and saw all of Joan's family photos lined up on her chest of drawers. A lifetime of memories, she pondered. When it comes down to it, we're all the same, making memories with our families to look back on when we're old and grey.

Gradually, she noticed without the confines of the physical body, if she concentrated, she was able to stretch her whole being out, nearly filling the room, and it felt marvellous. She was too nervous to stretch any further, although she felt she could have stretched out the entire length of the house, maybe even further. She felt such a deep sense of peace as she did so. It was like she was connected to the air that was all around everything; like she was part of the air that you breathe. She wondered if maybe she could be breathed in by someone, if she got too close to them and drifted a little further away from Joan, just in case. She had never thought much about the space that's around you, around objects, around matter. But in this moment, she felt as if she was that space, part of everything that is, part of nature seeping back into the atmosphere. It was such a wonderful experience, so deeply moving to feel part of everything.

With this renewed sense of being, she started to get a bit cocky and wondered if she would be able to move down to the nurse's station and see who was on duty. Quick as a flash, like the time before, she found herself hovering over the nurse's desk. Amazing, she thought, I just need to think of a place and I'm there. She was taken aback at the speed and how effortless it was to get there. It had been such a long time that she had done anything at speed that it was taking a while to get used to it. She looked down and could see Jane was on duty tonight. She could see her just coming out of one of the resident's bedrooms and was sitting back down at her desk. She picked up a pen and started to write. Her long blonde hair was pinned up in a bun, with a few wispy bits starting to fall down around her face. Grace didn't get to see Jane very much, as she covered nights and Grace was normally asleep by the time Jane checked in on her. But the few times they had spoken she seemed very nice. She was a tall, willowy lady and had mentioned how working nights fitted in well with her childcare, as her husband was able to look after the children. Grace wondered if Jane had any sense at all that she was there, hovering over her head. But if she did, she never looked up. Grace noticed that Jane had a beautiful pale green aura around her body; it was quite mesmerising to watch. She looked at the way the aura moved with her body as her hand migrated from side to side when writing. How beautiful the human body actually is, thought Grace. She'd never really taken the time to think about it before. How perfectly created we are, everything in our body is so finely balanced and tuned. Now she was without a body she could see how separated we actually are from our body. We have been led to believe that we are our body, but that is so untrue, she discovered. Our body really is a magnificent machine to store our spirit in, she realised. Without our bodies we would not be able to feel the wind on our faces or the light touch of someone's fingers. It was then that she realised that she didn't really feel any of those sensations like she did when she was in her body. Everything felt so light and the only thing she felt physically was herself vibrating gently. She didn't know whether she was hot or cold. She couldn't smell the faint odour of cleaning products, or worse still, the faint smell of urine that sometimes wafted round the rooms. Everything was now more intense but in an emotional sense. She had that overwhelming feeling of peace and love which seemed to take over all of the senses. How nostalgic she felt over the loss of her body; yet excited to feel without it at the same time. Being dead was proving to be such an extraordinary experience. If only people knew how wonderful it would feel. She drifted on further, moving up and down the corridors as she slowly got used to using her thoughts to get her places. She just had to think of being somewhere and there she was. She visualised the sitting room downstairs and instantly found herself there, floating round the various Parker Knoll chairs. It was dark in the sitting room but amazingly she was able to see everything perfectly clearly. Her eyesight was incredible, better than she'd ever been able to see. The fact she could see all around her still amazed her. It made her feel as if she had superpowers. How very ordinary and limiting to only be able to see in front of you, she mused.

Now she was actually dead, she wondered what would

happen when they told James. As she thought of him, she found herself instantly staring down at him in his bed. Lying there next to Amanda, sound asleep. She hoped he would be OK. She moved down nearer to be close to him. She could see his chest rising up and down as he breathed. She could also see his beautiful blue aura with flecks of gold, sparkling all over his body. It reminded her of a time she had visited a medium who had told Grace she had a blue/green aura, with flecks of gold all around her too. The medium wanted to know what the flecks of gold were, but Grace was unable to answer her as she didn't really know anything about auras. She wished now she'd looked into it a bit more. But here was James with the same aura that was described to her. The gold flecks were beautiful. They almost made James look ethereal, like some sort of angel. As she moved closer to him, she felt his energy start to merge with hers and she felt an overwhelming rush of love explode through her body. Wow! That was amazing. She moved back slightly, as she didn't want to wake him and she was still a bit unsure of whether she could be sucked in with the breath. She noticed that he started to stir from the impact of their merging. Well, it was hardly surprising if he did stir.

It was such a powerful volt through her being, and she wondered what it felt like inside his body. She floated about a little while longer. She could see the sun was starting to creep in through the curtains and she wondered how long she had been out of her body. She realised that time didn't seem to play a part now that she was dead. She had no idea of time. It was just a case of being NOW. Being in this precise moment, instead of being a series of linear events like we have in the physical body. It was just a collection of NOWs. It was as if instead of 'time' passing 'through' us, like when in the physical body, in the spiritual body, 'you' move 'through time' and time stands still. She wondered if that's why sometimes people in shock, or after encountering a really shocking experience like a car crash, would say things like 'time slowed down' or 'time stood still'. Very strange, it was such an odd but also familiar feeling, she thought.

She toyed with the idea of moving on as she didn't want to be there when James woke. Just as she was considering it, she became aware of a beautiful circle of light starting to appear before her. It started off as just a tiny pinprick of light. Then it started to get bigger and bigger; the light starting to get brighter and brighter as it swirled round in a clockwise direction, like a spinning vortex that was sideways on. The light was so bright it would have blinded the human eye, but instead, for Grace, it kept her transfixed. She was almost hypnotised by it. She then began to feel a pulsation emanating from the light, driving right through her and drawing her towards it in a gravitational pull. She could sense an even stronger feeling of love and peace starting to flood her being, hooking her and pulling her in. She found herself totally surrendering to the light; allowing it to swallow her up whole, as she gently, yet with purpose, started to make her way towards the light. As she did so, once inside, she found herself catapulted through a tunnel of light. There were flashes of what looked like lightning bolts exploding as she flew past them. She felt like she was on a giant roller coaster. It was so thrilling that excitement coursed through her, giving her little shock waves of pleasure. She had no fear at all. She felt totally safe and protected and loved. Never before had she felt so alive, which was ironic, considering she was dead. She had such a rush of adrenaline; she didn't want it to end. It was the most wonderful experience she'd ever known. She felt as if she was being reborn again, travelling down the birth canal. What a thought, she mused. Imagine dying being the same process as being born. Maybe that's what's happening, maybe I'm being born into heaven. That would shock a lot of people.

As she started to gather speed, she could see that there was a darkness starting to show at the end of the tunnel. She wasn't expecting the darkness. She had heard that there would be a light. She felt as if she had been joined by a higher presence on either side of her; a rush of love starting to envelop her, and she felt a pair of wings wrap around her. Just before she hit the darkness, the light changed to a glowing amber colour and then she was surrounded by the shadows. It was not scary; it was like a warm, soothing cocoon of inky blackness, cushioning her landing. Still the wings continued to wrap tightly around her, allowing her to float, swaddled in this unconditional love, rather like a baby wrapped in its mother's arms after it's born. Such an ecstatic feeling of complete love and serenity! There were no thoughts, no pictures, coming into her mind, just complete, blissful nothingness, surrounding her and running through her, as if she had merged and become the inky blackness too. She was just a shapeless form without a body, dissolving in this ocean of darkness, aware of the surrender of her being to this space but feeling totally at ease and safe with the process. She marvelled at how wonderful this dying business was and thought she would happily stay here for the whole of eternity, slowly drifting into what felt like a deep, long sleep.

As she floated on in this cocooned inky blackness, she started to feel a shift in her surroundings. She sensed the darkness falling away from her and the light start to filter in. The soothing confinements of those beautiful wings started to unwrap her, as beautiful bright colours surrounded her. As she was getting used to her bearings, she realised that very gently she was being put down in the most beautiful meadow she had ever seen. It was full of wildflowers with bright vivid colours. Some colours she didn't recognise as she had never seen them before on Earth. There were enormous butterflies with the most beautiful patterns fluttering amongst the flowers, as well giant bees busily collecting their nectar. She was astounded at the beauty of the auras that were surrounding everything. The sky was covered in beautiful hues of purples and lavenders and there was an enormous lilac sun shining down upon her. She felt more alive than she had ever felt before. It was as if she was connected to everything and was able to communicate with everything, like they were all powered from one incredible source.

At the bottom of the meadow was a little woodland. She noticed lots of bright little gold sparks flying about between the trees. Towards the right of the meadow was an enormous oak tree standing proudly, emitting the most glorious shimmers of light from its branches. It must have been thousands of years old. She'd never seen a tree so huge before. She knew that some of the trees in Canada could grow to huge heights, but this tree was taller than any she had seen. It was impossible to see the top; it was endless and went right up into the sky. It was awesome and gave off the most wonderful ripples of unconditional love that flowed straight into her energy field, making her quiver with sheer joy and happiness. As she started to move and float around the tree, some animals came into view. A beautiful tiger was prowling the meadow, but what was strange was that it was walking amongst other animals like deer, badgers and other woodland creatures which normally would be its prey. However, there was no fear shown from any of the animals; they just seemed to be happy to move around each other quite casually. How bizarre to see a tiger placed in such an unusual setting. Grace had no fear of it either; the place was so serene and calm it was impossible to feel anything other than a sense of peace and wonder. It was mind-blowing, she didn't think it could get any better than this. She drifted slowly around, admiring the beauty. She could hear a little stream running through the woodland and went over to investigate. It was so strange to float rather than walk. She enjoyed the freedom it gave her. The lightness she felt was incredible. She could swoop up and down, go fast or slow, and to see everything from a 360-degree panoramic view was amazing.

She wanted to check out the little stream, and instantly found herself in the woodland, looking at the little stream flowing between the trees which had beautiful gold and silver flecks sparkling from it. She noticed the gold sparks she saw earlier were actually little orbs of light flitting between the trees. They looked as if they were little sprites or fairies; maybe they were? Maybe fairies did exist after all? She once knew a lady who was convinced that there were fairies at the bottom of her garden. She would even speak to them and they would advise her on growing things in her garden. Grace wasn't so sure at the time. She was a nice lady and seemed perfectly compos mentis, but even to Grace, who believed in spirits and angels, it did seem a bit of a stretch to believe in fairies. That was for children's stories, wasn't it? But after seeing these beautiful orbs she was sure they were fairies or sprites or something like that.

She drifted back into the meadow and carried on enjoying the feeling of not having a body. It was immensely satisfying and liberating not being confined by a clumsy overcoat. She pondered over how cumbersome it was being in a physical body. It felt as though she must have been wearing a space suit and space boots when she walked the Earth, to help weigh her down so she didn't drift off into the ether. Being here made walking on the Earth seem like wading through treacle. Everything here was so light and fast. Again, everything she thought seemed to happen or appear to her immediately, as if she was creating what was happening. Even when she was wondering about the stream, she seemed to instantly be there. She was enjoying discovering and using these new gifts. She wished she could have done this on Earth. What fun she would have had then.

She moved over to the oak tree to soak up more of its gorgeous energies. She floated around the tree, bathing in its radiance and as she did so little ripples of ecstasy moved up and down her like little electric shocks.

Then quite suddenly, she startled. Intuitively she felt a change about to occur and 'felt' rather than 'saw' a light coming into view. Across the meadow she could see another pinprick of light approach her. Just like before, it started to grow larger and turn into another vortex of light. Instead of being pulled into it though, she felt as if energies were coming out of it. She moved in closer to take a look, but her feelings were inexplicably starting to change to those of overwhelming excitement. She had no idea what was happening on a conscious level, but her feelings were definitely reacting on an unconscious level. Thrills of excitement were coursing through her being, as she continued to watch and feel this spinning vortex getting bigger and bigger. Just as she thought she was about to spontaneously combust, the vortex started to change to a wider circle of light that stopped spinning. As it moved closer, the light got bigger and bigger and started to change into what looked like a crowd of human forms coming towards her. As quick as the forms started to appear, they began to morph into what looked like people with hair and faces and clothes. They all had the same bluey/ green auras with flecks of gold shimmering around them. Incredibly, before she could make out who they were, her being reacted before her mind did. She knew these were her kin, her loved ones, and she instantly found herself waiting eagerly in front of them, watching as they clearly came into focus. Quickly she found herself scanning the crowd of people with her mind and her heart. Shivers of longing and excitement were rippling up and down her energy field, as she spotted her beloved son and husband, along with her mother and father, her sisters Catherine and Louise, as well as all sorts of aunts, uncles, friends from the past, and neighbours. For a fleeting instant, she thought she caught sight of an old classmate who had bullied her terribly at school. But that was quickly forgotten with the overwhelming rush of love that took over her. So long had she waited for this moment, thirty-eight years to be precise, to be reunited with her son. She was astounded at how young and healthy they all looked. Her husband looked a similar age to her son. He had a full shock of dark hair, the same as when she first met him. He was a very handsome man, naturally very broad and muscular. All the girls were after him, she couldn't believe her luck when he asked her out on a date. He had piercing blue eyes, passed on from his Irish descendants, his mother used to say. She used to go weak at the knees when she looked into them; she felt as if she could see right down into his soul. Standing right beside him was their son Michael. He was taller than his father but not as broad, however he was just as handsome but in a completely different way. He had the same thick, dark glossy hair that his father had. He took after Grace's side of the family with his olive skin and brown eyes. Apparently, one of her ancestors, her great-grandmother, was a Romany gypsy. She thought the olive skin and brown eyes probably originated from her line. Without waiting a moment longer, she leaped forward into the crowd, almost diving into them. There was a beautiful moment of elation, relief and love that flooded into her very soul. She felt like a person dying of thirst who had just experienced their first droplet of water.

'Oh Michael, my son, you beautiful boy, how I have waited for you for so long!' She then turned to John without letting go of Michael. 'John, you look so young. How I have dreamed of this moment, my darling.' Thoughts and feelings were flashing across her being. Words were being spoken but not by the tongue. Everything was telepathically spoken, or more accurately, spoken with feelings.

'Hello Ma,' said Michael. 'It's been a long time for you I know, I'm sorry Ma.' He paused, 'I'm so sorry that you have been so sad for so long. But I promise you Ma, I've never left your side or Dad's or James's. I've seen it all, I've been there through everything. For me, it's like I've only been away for a heartbeat. I'm just so sorry that it's seemed like forever for you. But I'm here now with you and I promise everything will be fine; all is as it's supposed to be. I will tell you everything. You are safe. I love you so much.' His words were implanted into her being with such tenderness and love. Every word sent in thought was like a gentle caress all over her energy field. Michael's were the only words spoken to her through thought; with John and the rest of the crowd everything was communicated through feeling.

Grace couldn't get over how young and well everyone looked. She had noticed a man standing away from the group who was dressed in a white robe. He looked as though he would have fitted in well around the time of Jesus. He had a brilliant white light shining around him, with a gentle smile on his face and a radiance of sheer love and wisdom that emanated from him. She recognised him but could not think where from. Her curiosity soon got lost in the moment as she was so overwhelmed with seeing her loved ones, but thought she would ask Michael and John about him later.

It seemed like forever that she was able to bathe in everyone's glorious energy, soaking it up like a sponge. She felt gentle healing taking place to her bruised and battered heart, as if it was being rebuilt. She felt the wholeness start to come back to it, as its cracks and rawness were being soothed and caressed. She surrendered totally into the moment, enjoying the feeling of being complete and whole, at one with all her kin. But it felt different to how she felt when she was first born into heaven.

When she was floating in the inky blackness, she had felt as if she was part of everything, that there was no individual Grace, that she was melded into the ether and was part of the cosmos. Now she felt more like an individual that was being melded with her family, to create this collective group of beings. She instinctively felt the strong connection to everyone and had emotional interactions with them all, but simultaneously. It reminded her of the conversations that her grandchildren used to have on that Zoom thingy, where everyone can talk at once. But here the conversations were all done through feelings and with such clarity.

She was dwelling on why she felt such a difference to when she first arrived in the inky blackness, when Michael interrupted her thought.

'That's because, when you're first born into heaven, you are met by 'All That Is' or God, or whatever you want to call it. You are part of 'All That Is' and you are born back into your natural state of being,' said Michael. Grace was startled: one, because of what Michael had said, and two, because how did he know what she was thinking.

'How did you know what I was thinking, Michael?' she said, stunned.

'Because Ma, we communicate differently in heaven. It's all done through telepathy and through feeling. No one ever gets confused with what one is wanting to say or feeling. There is complete transparency here. Only the truth is shared. We are living in such a high vibration there is no room for lies or deceit or hidden meanings, like there is when we speak words in the human form,' he laughed.

'Gosh that's so clever,' she said. 'It makes us seem so basic and...'

'Unevolved,' said Michael finishing her sentence.

'Well, yes, exactly. It makes me wonder how we ever got by at all really, using words to communicate.'

'Well, it certainly makes life harder, or it did for me, especially when there are no words to describe how you're feeling and there's no other way to communicate other than in actions. It can cause a whole lot of trouble,' he said, then paused. 'But, let's not get too deep into that just yet, you've only just arrived. Listen Ma, don't worry but Dad and the others are going to leave us for a short while, but the good news is you're coming to spend some time with me.'

She turned to John. 'John, where are you going?' she said as she felt him start to fade away along with the others.

'It's OK Ma, trust me, you will see them again but they've gone back to continue with their work. It's difficult for you to understand at the moment but they were just essences of themselves that left 'All That Is' to greet you and show their love. You will catch up with them soon but for now you are with me. I'm going to be your guide until you get settled in. I've been here longer than Dad and I'm further ahead in the process than he is, so it was decided that I would have the pleasure of your company.'

As he spoke, Michael was grinning at her with the same cheeky smile that he always had and he knew darn well that she found his smile irresistible. He was always able to wrap her round his little finger. 'I do trust you,' said Grace. 'It's just, I'm a little disappointed. I was hoping to spend more time with your father too, as well as with you.'

'You will Ma, soon, just not quite yet. For now, we're going to leave this place and go to somewhere different.'

Grace was intrigued. 'I thought this was it, Michael. Where else are we going?' She was a bit hesitant but Michael pressed on and reassured her.

'It's OK Ma, you've been to this place before. Do you remember when you connected with me during your dreams and meditations?'

'Yes, I do,' she replied and straight away felt a whooshing sensation as she felt herself instantly transported there.

Chapter 3

Michael's Heaven

She found herself looking out at a familiar view – a large beautiful sparkling lake with crystal clear waters. In the background was an enormous range of mountains, standing strong and proud with snow caps on the very peaks. At the shore of the lake was a wooden cabin, with a veranda out the front and a forest of pine trees edging round the lake. She had seen this place many times before.

'Welcome to my little piece of heaven Ma,' said Michael.

As he moved towards the cabin, she noticed a beautiful black Labrador come bounding round the corner of the cabin to greet her. She instantly recognised him as Harvey; he had belonged to Michael's best friend. Harvey had died very soon after Michael; she had seen him with Michael many times during her dreams, but she had assumed she had made it up. She knew how much Michael had loved Harvey, and she thought it was her way of comforting herself. Michael was never allowed a dog as he was allergic to them; but he was mad about dogs and he was devastated that he was never allowed to have one. She recalled the times he used to beg her, even though he came out in terrible hives. She knew that whenever he stayed at his best friend's house, he'd be all over Harvey; so, she used to dose him up with antihistamines.

'No, Ma, this is real, you didn't make it up. You really did connect with me, and Harvey really did come to join me in heaven. Animals can do that you know, when they pass. If you choose to have them, and the pet wants to join you – which they normally do – then you can create it and make it happen.'

She smiled inwardly at the way he had answered the question she was thinking, without her necessarily directing the question to him. It was going to take a little while to adjust to Michael being able to know everything that goes on in her mind, she thought.

'Don't worry, you'll get used to it, remember it works both ways,' he laughed, and gentle ripples went up and down her energy field with his laughter.

Grace was quite overwhelmed with emotion. 'I'm just so happy that this is where you ended up, and that I was not just imagining it. I used to think it was my mind playing tricks on me just to ease my pain. This place is so breathtaking, I can't tell you the joy it gave me imagining you here.' She started to move around the place, exploring everywhere like a child. 'Is this where you live with your father?' she asked gently.

'Nope. This is my little piece of heaven, the same as

the meadow was your little piece of heaven. I come here on my own whenever I feel like it.' He moved closer to her. 'You're confused I can tell, let me explain. We are ultimately creators. Yes, we are spiritual beings made of energy, but we are also creators. What we don't realise when we're human, is that we have the ability to create everything that happens to us, and we do. We just don't realise it. Before I died, I used to think of heaven in my subconscious as this place, the same as you used to think of the meadow as your place. When you die, the first process you go through, after you have been met by 'All That Is', is to create your version of heaven, so that you have an element of control over what is happening to you. There is far more to come, it is a lot more complex, and in time you will see, but for now you can experience your heaven, or in this case my heaven.'

She was silent for a while, then pondered, 'How come I'm in your heaven and not mine then?'

'Good question Ma, that's because you did create this heaven too, because you knew about it in your dreams when you connected with me. So, part of your heaven is the meadow, but the other part of your heaven is here, thanks to me!'

'So, what happens if people don't believe in heaven, or God, what happens then?' she asked.

'Well, if they don't believe in heaven, they will find themselves drifting in a nothingness for a short while. Not the same as when you're in the inky blackness; you'll just float around in the nothing for a bit, because that's what your mind has created. When it's time for your loved ones to come to greet you, they will draw you out of the nothingness, and one of your family will be there to guide you, like I am being with you. The same as if someone thought they were going to hell, which incidentally doesn't exist, but if they thought it did, they could create a hell for them to arrive in. But it wouldn't harm them in any way, they would just become the observer of their own hell, until such time that their loved ones would come to greet them. They would then gently explain to them that it was not real, and they would guide them into the next process.'

'Oh, I see! Or at least I think understand. It's so beautiful here, I can see why you come here to be on your own, although I just assumed you would be with everyone else, altogether,' Grace said, moving over to the log cabin to be beside Michael.

'Well, you can be if you want to, or you can choose to have some timeout on your own, whatever suits you really. When I first crossed over, I came here quite a bit, just to be close to you really. But also to reflect on how things had gone in my life. Obviously, I had quite a bit to think about,' he laughed gently.

Grace hesitated, then eventually spoke. 'I wasn't sure how heaven would take someone who took their own life, because, well, you know what the Catholics think about that sort of thing.'

'Yes, I do Ma, but that really isn't the case here.

There were a lot of factors that were taken into account, and you will get to find out all of them in time, or at least understand things from a bigger picture,' he said softly.

Grace went on to say, 'I never realised you were that unhappy, that you would even think of leaving us like that. I knew you were very deep in your thinking, but you had a loving family, a lovely girlfriend, wonderful friends, I just don't really understand why you did what you did, I guess that's what I'm trying to say.' She was surprised she was having such a deep conversation with Michael on such an emotive subject, without feeling the heavy pain that often burdened her heart. She felt light, upbeat and full of joy and happiness. The whole conversation seemed quite surreal.

'Well, the only way to describe it to you was I felt as if I didn't belong on the Earth; like I had been brought into the wrong world. Of course, I was happy with you guys, but as I grew older, I realised what a horrible world it was, at the time, I didn't see the beauty of any of it. I felt as if I was living under a dark, oppressive cloud that was pushing down on me. I couldn't think of anything other than escaping this darkness that followed me everywhere. When I first passed, I felt such elation and lightness; I was overjoyed at being released from that pain. I never thought about what would happen to everyone that I left behind; I was so absorbed in my own pain, and for that I'm truly sorry. As I went through my life review, so many things became clear to me concerning why I behaved the way I did; especially when I realised that it was part of my life plan to experience poor mental health,' he said.

'You've totally lost me now, what do you mean life review? Life plan? What's that got to do with you taking your own life?' she questioned.

'Sorry Ma, I'm going too quickly for you I know. I'll try to slow it down.' He paused for a while, then continued, 'OK, when you cross over, and you've met with your family, and experienced some time in the heaven that you have created, you are then be met by an ascended master. I don't know whether you saw him, but our soul family has an ascended master, attached to our group. An ascended master is a highly evolved spirit who is helping with the evolvement of others. Some ascended masters have lived on the Earth and some haven't. You may have seen our ascended master in his human form; he was in a white robe, with a beautiful golden light surrounding him.'

'Yes, I did see him!' said Grace 'I wondered who he was, he looked so familiar, but seemed as if he should be living in the times of the Bible.'

'Yes, that's right Ma, he did live in the time of Jesus, and he was one of the disciples. But don't get too caught up on the Bible, it's been so badly corrupted and changed; meanings have been misinterpreted, as well as the greatest crime ever committed, with Mary Magdalene being portrayed as nothing more than a prostitute! In time, you will come to know the truth, I'm sure Oto will explain. The reason you recognised him, is because you have seen him many times before, in heaven. You may have also seen him in your dreams, as he would have been guiding you when you were on Earth, like a spirit guide.' He moved closer to Grace to gauge whether she had grasped everything he had said so far. When he felt confident that she had, he continued, 'So our ascended master will then spend some time with you, and take you to the halls of healing; it's the place where you go to connect with your base-self, and go through your life review.

'Before I explain about the life review, let me explain a bit about your base-self first. So, at the moment, you still think of yourself in human form, and that's OK to do so. You've recently passed and it's OK to think like that. That's the reason why you saw all of your loved ones in human form, and that we are still in human form now, pretty much. Soon, once you have reconnected with your base-self, you will truly experience yourself in your natural state, in spirit form. In spirit form, we are neither male nor female; we also have a spirit name, which is the name of our true-self, which you will soon discover. Our base-self houses the higher-self that stays in heaven, whilst essences of the soul split off into different lives, which incarnate on Earth. We incarnate onto the Earth to experience love, through relationships, as well as being able to express ourselves and evolve into the grandest versions of ourselves. After this, we return to heaven, and merge back with our base-self, bringing a wealth of knowledge, empathy and compassion, to nourish and grow the soul.' He paused to check whether Grace was still with him. He could see she was trying to grasp the concept, so he went on some more. 'When we incarnate on the Earth we already know a lot about the cast of characters that are around us, in other words we choose our parents, brother, sisters, etc. We even choose our nemesis! All of the characters are mainly from our soul family, and we all give our blessings to play different parts and different characters. Once we have agreed on the cast and characters, we live those lives over and over, again and again, until we evolve to the grandest versions of ourselves. That's why we have déjà vu, because we remember being somewhere, in a different lifetime, but with the same characters; we can link to these lives through our higher-selves.

Once we have reached this point, of being the grandest version of ourselves, we all change the cast and characters to new ones and start again. In other words, you have been my mother, and I your son, many, many times before, and you will be again, as we have still not reached full maturity. So, in effect I've never really left any of you, it was just a different version of this story. The next story will be different. You've watched me grow into an adult and live many lives with wives and children, and you will know that to be true when you merge back to your base-self. In this particular life it was important for me to experience poor mental health, and it was important for you to experience loss and grief. We all have free will in our lives though, so if we want to go against our life plan we can. That's usually when we feel unhappy though, because we are not following our gut instinct. Many people do take their own lives and some go against their life plan. It means they come back too early; but it's not frowned on here like people think, or the Catholics lead you to believe. It is kind of like a wasted opportunity though, so when that happens, it's more like the person kicks themselves for leaving too early, but nobody else will give you a hard time, they will help you through the process, and hopefully learn lessons for next time. However, in my case, it was part of my life plan.' He was quiet for a while, allowing Grace some time to take in all of this information.

She could sense he was waiting for a response, so she urged him to continue. 'Ma, I'm going to use an analogy to help you see things in a simpler way. Imagine, Grace Sullivan as a book, and every page of that book is a different life that Grace Sullivan has lived. A bit like Groundhog Day, but the lives will always be different, and the cast and characters are always the same. When you get to the end of that book, imagine another book, where you will play a different character, with a different name, maybe you will be a male, and of different colour or creed. Now, the pages of that book are the same character that lives life, over and over again, until it reaches the grandest version it can be. Then imagine another book, with a different character and different casts. Now imagine the library that houses those books; that library is the soul, your soul! And the books are all the different lives you have led as different people.'

He paused. 'Are you with me so far?'

'Yes, I think I am,' said Grace.

'Good. Now imagine, an infinite number of libraries, which represent endless beings, all feeding into one all-encompassing library, 'All That Is'. Think of all that knowledge and wisdom, all of those experiences that reside within everything. We are all part of that all-encompassing library; we all feed into it. That library is all that there is, there is nothing else that exists, except that library, split into many different forms. 'All That Is' is energy of the highest and purest form; it is so pure that for it to know itself it has to split off into many parts, so that it can experience and express itself, over and over again.

'Imagine if everything was always good and perfect in your life, how would you know it was good and perfect? You only know by comparing it to something that isn't good or isn't perfect. Hence, the reason we have duality on the Earth dimension, in other words, we have good and bad. For ultimately, there is only good; there is only the perfect energy of 'All That Is'. But to experience itself, the Earth was created, with its duality, allowing us to incarnate onto the Earth, with the gift of free will; that enables us to create, and express, and experience ourselves, in turn building up lifetimes of knowledge, wisdom, compassion and understanding. Allowing us to evolve to the grandest version we can be; only then will we permanently return to 'All That Is' and enjoy the wonder, and bliss, of floating into the depths of its ecstasy.'

There was silence between them for a while.

'That is absolutely mind-blowing!' Grace said, breaking the silence. 'It's just so incredible, it's like I'm Alice in Wonderland, and I've just fallen down the rabbit hole.'

'I know, it's so cool, right! It took me a while to get my head round it. Once you merge with your base-self, everything will become crystal clear. At the moment it's like being in a bit of a fog,' he said.

As he spoke, Grace mused over his terminology and said mockingly, 'Since when did you start to use the term cool? You sound like the kids, I can't remember you speaking like that.'

'That's because I'm around my great nieces and nephews all the time Ma, it's well sick!'

With that, they both roared with laughter, as their energy fields expanded in and out and they merged together, just enjoying each other's company and the feeling of oneness at being reunited.

Grace took time to process everything that Michael had just said, then after some thought said, 'You've spoken about the base-self, but what about the life review?'

'Ah! The life review, well, here goes. Before we are born, we have a life plan, or contract, as some people like to call it. The soul family, and our ascended masters, as well as the elders, who are like a panel of very highly evolved ascended masters, all decide what life would be beneficial for our evolvement. We all decide what would bring most value and fulfilment to ourselves and the family. We don't decide exact details, as that would spoil the fun and creativity, but we have a basic concept of what we want to achieve in the life we are about to be born into. It takes a lot of consideration and is well thought out; it's a lot more complex than it sounds, but there is also a simplicity to it. We even know exit dates, that we can use to leave the Earth. In other words, dates we can choose to die. When we are born, we have champions in the form of ascended masters, spirit guides, angels as well as our higher-self, all helping to guide us, to make sure we follow the life plan. We call it on Earth, our gut instinct or intuition. When we follow these instincts, or follow the middle path, as some spiritual gurus call it on the Earth, we feel more fulfilled, more peaceful and content. If only we knew how many entities there were, willing us on, watching over us, loving us; more than we can ever imagine. We are never alone, there is so much love out there for us, if only we knew how to connect to it. You were great Ma, you connected easily; your vibration was always so high on the Earth, you were easy to connect to. Some people though, they are operating at such a low vibration, it's really difficult for us to connect with them. But we are always there, waiting patiently, willing them on to make the right choices, sending out our love to them, hoping that they will feel it at some level.' He stopped to take stock, then continued.

'So, to sum it up, you're born onto the Earth to live out your life, following the life plan, which has been prearranged in heaven. Once you've lived your life and chosen which exit date you want to leave the Earth – which isn't a conscious choice incidentally – only the soul knows when the right time is to leave, you exit the Earth, and are born back into heaven. Once in heaven, after you've been met by 'All That Is', and spent time in your created heaven, you'll be met by your soul family, and then your ascended master will take you to merge with your base-self and have your life review. Now, this is the bit you've been waiting for. At your life review, you will flash through every part of your life in an instant. It will go through all your major events, but it will focus more on the type of person you have been. All of the good and bad deeds you have done, and the effect you have had on other people will be looked at, as well as the feelings or emotions it caused other people to have. The times that you've been hurt, either physically or emotionally by others, or the times you've hurt others, either physically or emotionally, will be examined and you'll re-live those moments and experience the ripple effects that those actions have caused. So, if you've been a kind person, you'll feel the good emotions that you gave to others a thousand-fold. But if you've been mean and cruel, you'll also experience the pain you've caused a thousand-fold. At the life review, it isn't about looking at material gain, whether you were rich or poor. It's about what type of person you were, how you interacted with others, how you regarded yourself. That's the crazy thing Ma, we spend so much of our human life trying to gain material things, thinking that's what defines us and makes us so important, when in fact it's not about that at all. If only we knew the wasted hours we spend being miserable, working in jobs that we hate, following the rules that society sets, like sheep. Brainwashed into thinking that we need to own our own house, have a big car, and wear expensive clothes and jewellery to be anyone in life. Instead, we should be spending time with our families. Going out into nature, exploring, creating and interacting with each other; building communities to share produce and amenities, instead of building fences to keep people out.

'Don't get me wrong, it's not about judging you as you have been led to believe by certain religious sectors. Because everyone in some of their lives would have been cruel or mean at some point, as they wouldn't have known any better. But, because of that experience, they will discover at their life review the pain they have caused to others, and therefore evolve to a better version of themselves for future lives.

'But let's just say some live reviews may feel better than others, but, the harder lives, are the ones where we do the most evolving, and that's celebrated in the life review too. It's more about what you have learned and remembered from the experience.

'When you can feel the full impact of how your actions affected others, it will stay with you for future lives. You will develop empathy and compassion. You can always tell the old souls on the Earth; they are the people who have empathy and compassion and patience. They are usually the most generous with their time and emotions, and lead a more simple way of life, preferring to keep to a small circle of friends. Do you remember Mr Salter, that strange-looking, trampy bloke that used to live in the woods?'

'Yes, I do remember him, he was a lovely man, he used to stop by and bring me flowers that he'd found when he was out foraging. People were so horrible about him though, calling him a tramp and crossing over when he came near. He lived in a little shack, didn't he? He used to say he preferred the company of the animals in the woodland to people,' she laughed, then went on to say, 'Sometimes, I had to completely agree with him.'

'Well, he is a really highly evolved spirit here; he teaches in the halls of healing, you'll go there soon. He was one of the first spirits after I passed to greet me; I was really shocked to see him, but after I had my life review, and everything became clearer, I could see how pure his soul was. He doesn't need to come back to Earth as he is vibrating on such a high level, but he came back for the fun of it, just to experience being in the physical again. Can you imagine that?' he said, thoughtfully.

'In a strange sort of way, I'm not surprised. He had a very comforting manner about him. I always used to feel good in his presence, I could never understand why people were so mean. I think it was because of the way that he chose to live, it was so different, so basic. People don't seem to like people being different, do they?' she said.

'Don't get me started on that one!' he laughed.

'What about the people who have been really evil, like serial killers etc.?' she questioned.

'Well, obviously you can imagine how their life review is going to go! They have more help in a way, they will have the assistance of higher evolved beings that can deal with that sort of thing. They are taken to the wilderness, or somewhere similar, where they will work intensely through what went wrong. Or how they went astray. They will suffer immensely in their life review, as you can imagine, but they will have intensive healing given to them. Remember, we are all one; all from the same source, and there will only ever be love. There will never be judgements made, the only spirits that will judge will be themselves by experiencing the pain of the life review.'

'Wow! That sounds pretty intense. It makes me shudder to think about it,' she said. She was quiet for a few moments, deep in thought, then said, 'Will I get to see more people soon? Or is it just limited to our soul family and ascended masters?'

'Definitely! Yes, you will. Soon you'll meet Oto, and he'll take you on the next part of your journey. But I'll be around so don't worry, and then we can catch up with Dad,' he said.

'I take it Oto is the name of our ascended master, the man in the white robe?' she added.

'Yes, that's his spiritual name. You'll find out your name when you merge with your base-self.'

'What's your spiritual name, then?' she replied.

'AHA!' he said dramatically, 'wouldn't you like to know? You'll find out all in good time,' he teased.

After that, they spent time exploring the lake, flying over the waters together, then speeding up the side of the mountains before chasing each other down. Both of their auras were expanded out and shining brightly, with sheer joy and happiness. Then eventually they would rest on the veranda, staring out at the glorious view.

'Oh, this has been wonderful,' Grace gushed. 'I've imagined this moment thousands of times in my head, and still, it comes nowhere close to the magic of the real thing. She nestled into his aura and little shockwaves of joy bounced up down her energy field, 'I can't think of anywhere more perfect I'd rather be than here, right now.'

'That's good Ma, because that's the only place you'll ever be, here, in the moment,' he answered.

Grace didn't reply, she didn't need to. She just stayed in this glorious moment, taking in the beauty of the wonderful feelings that were vibrating through her energy field, drifting into a blissful state of contentment.

Chapter 4

The Halls of Healing

M ichael brought her back from her self-induced daydream, for want of a better word. As she came round, she felt the familiar shift of energy start to change all around her. She then felt the spinning vortex of light, before she saw it appear in front of them. She was getting more used to this happening. She felt Michael's energy field expand with excitement as he was eagerly waiting for Oto to appear.

'Hold on to your seatbelts Ma! Oto is coming!' he laughed.

Suddenly she felt a boom of energy explode through her energy field upon his arrival. It was like a bomb going off, with a tsunami of waves flooding into her energy field. It felt as though energy was being cannonballed out of the vortex towards her. As she continued to watch, she could see his human shape come into view as his features started to appear more clearly. He was still wearing the same white robe that he had on earlier. He looked as if he was in his late twenties, maybe early thirties. He had dark hair and a dark beard, his skin was olive and his eyes were dark brown, almost black in colour. He was quite a handsome man and had the most beautiful golden glow surrounding his whole body, with fireworks of gold sparking off around his aura. His smile was mesmerising and Grace felt completely overwhelmed by his presence; he was giving off such a powerful vibe, she felt rooted to the spot. As the vortex disappeared, he moved towards them and spoke gently using telepathy as well as feelings to communicate.

'Greetings beloved one, how pleased I am to see your return.' He moved in closer and fixed his eyes on Grace. 'I can see how happy you are to be reunited with your son once again. The Earth years are very long and I know it was a difficult time for you being separated.' His voice was deep and powerful but at the same time very soothing and comforting.

Grace was unsure what to say so kept her answer short. 'Yes, it was.'

'You must be feeling a bit overwhelmed by everything at the moment, but rest assured everything will become clearer after you have merged with your base-self as Michael no doubt has told you,' he said.

'Yes, Michael has been filling me in with everything, it's a lot to take on board. However, it does slowly seem to be sounding very familiar,' she said shyly.

'That will be the knowing that resides within you, blessed one. You are starting to remember the miracle of life and the journey you are upon.' He turned to Michael and embraced him with a sort of energy hug; sparks were going off all over the place.

'Greetings Ata, love and light to you,' he said, pausing as they continued the strange energy hug. Grace noticed that when Michael was near Oto his aura expanded and grew brighter as if he was soaking up Oto's energy. Michael had never looked so well, she thought. Feelings of pride cascaded up and down in little fizzing motions, throughout her energy field.

Oto continued to speak to Michael. 'You have done well. I know this was important to you and you have worked hard to make sure this was a smooth transition for your mother.'

'Thank you,' said Michael. 'I couldn't be happier and was pleased that you had faith in me.'

'Well of course,' replied Oto. 'Why wouldn't I? You have worked hard and reaped the rewards.'

Oto turned to Grace. 'Michael has explained to you that you will spend some time with me in the halls of healing. After you have merged, you will have a time of further healing and learning. Then you will return once more to Michael and also to John and the rest of your soul family. Once again, there will be a joyful reunion, only this time you will remember what your life plan was and what you have achieved in your evolution. But for now, it is time to bid your farewells.'

He was very direct in his words, telling her what was going to happen, but it was surprisingly reassuring and

Grace was strangely ready for this. An excitement had started to grow within her and she knew that she was safe and that Oto spoke the truth. She knew her son would be waiting for her once more to help her continue on the next part of her journey. She turned towards Michael. No words were needed, she leaned in for the same energy hug that she had seen Oto give Michael. She felt his warm embrace and the loving energies flooding throughout her being. They communicated everything they needed to say in feelings then released each other gently as Grace moved towards Oto.

Before she felt the energies start to shift as Oto leaned in to merge with her, she quickly turned to Michael and cheekily said, 'See you soon Ata!' and with that she felt a sudden whoosh of energy as she felt herself catapulted at lightning speed through another vortex. Only this time she felt as if she was inside a tornado, the force of energy was immense. She felt herself tumbling all over the place but felt safe and secure inside Oto's protected energy.

Oto's words brought her round from the power of it all as he suddenly announced, 'We are here, beloved one.'

As he gently released her from his energies, she was met by the most incredible view she had ever seen. She found herself in the most beautiful garden looking up at a magnificent building. It was enormous with great stone pillars and marble steps leading up to the front of it. The walls were vibrating and changing colours intermittently, they looked fluid, like ripples of water but you couldn't see through them. There was a dome of golden light above the building, sending out shimmering beams of gold into the lavender sky above. In the garden located at the front of the building was an elaborate water fountain with water flecked with silver and gold cascading down it. It reminded her of the gardens of Versailles but far more colourful and beautiful. Around the gardens were gorgeous, perfectly shaped roses of the most vivid colours she had ever seen. Some of the colours she had never seen before, they were incredible; it was an overload to the senses. It was as if she could smell and taste the colours without having a mouth to taste or a nose to smell them. Her whole being felt lighter and her energy was expanding out to soak up the whole environment. Once more she saw the enormous butterflies and bees flying round, weaving in and out of the flowers. But what she found most incredible were the huge rainbow-coloured orbs of light zipping around with lightning speed. She knew these to be spirits. Every now and then they would remain still or slow down for her to see beautiful energy fields of the brightest rainbow colours, with a white light shining through the centre causing the colours to turn pastel behind. Each spirit was different in colour and shone brightly with their own unique colours. They were the most beautiful beings she had ever seen. She felt her centre start to swell and she found herself instinctively stretching and expanding out, trying to reach out to the spirits as they dashed past her. She felt like she was magnetised and as they whizzed past her, they were pulling her towards them. It was such a powerful feeling, a rush of excitement, she couldn't stop herself from reacting. A force other than her mind was taking over her and she loved it and didn't want the feeling to stop.

'You are feeling the power of connectedness, of being one with all others. On Earth you feel the illusion of separation. But not here, here we know our truth that we are all from source, 'All That Is'.' Oto started to move towards the building so Grace quickly followed. When they reached the water fountain he stopped and paused in front of it, continuing to speak as Grace stared transfixed at the intricate detailing of the fountain, mesmerised by its gold and silver flecked water tumbling down gracefully over the smooth granite stone.

'In order to understand things on a deeper level you need to appreciate the whole picture. As Michael explained 'All That Is' is pure consciousness at the highest level. There is nothing else. Everything that ever was and ever will be is 'All That Is', there cannot be anything else. Now imagine an energy so powerful, so pure operating at the highest vibration possible. You felt my energy like a powerful explosion, now imagine that an infinite number of times greater,' he said.

Grace struggled to imagine that, it was quite overwhelming. 'That would be a mighty powerful force of energy indeed!' she said.

'Precisely,' he said. 'For 'All That Is' to experience itself and in turn experience pure love it needed to have the illusion of separation so that it may truly know and love itself. So 'All That Is' divided up a part of itself into tiny particles. Imagine a droplet of water from the ocean. Each droplet of water is a spirit created. So now 'All That Is' can experience itself and love itself through us, through our experiences and relationships. Each droplet of water has come from 'All That Is' the great ocean of pure consciousness, which makes our spirit pure consciousness vibrating at the highest level. It is totally untouched by negativity or any dark source as it is pure love from 'All That Is' that cannot be tarnished, corrupted or destroyed…

'So now we have the illusion of separation. But for 'All That Is' to experience oneself as pure love even as separate it needs to be able to exist at a lower vibration to incarnate onto the Earth realm, so the soul was created. The soul is the non-physical energy that makes up the part of who you are. It's a vehicle of energy which is able to travel from life to life, building up layers of experiences and emotions which in turn will also carry scars and traumas, which is carried forward from one life into the next and the next and the next for as long as required. The soul craves to merge back into 'All That Is' and is driven to raise its vibration through the process of evolution to return once more to the higher realms. So blessed one, the meaning of life is to understand and experience love.' Oto paused and remained silent for a few moments so Grace could digest the information, then continued.

'The soul decides what lifetimes it needs to help with

its evolution. As you have already discovered, we have soul families which help each other on the journey, by taking on different casts and characters.' He turned to face Grace. 'Sometimes the characters are not always loving and kind towards you. If the soul needs to experience something in particular, a member of your soul family may agree to be the person who turns out to be your nemesis. Or you may have agreed to play that part for someone too.'

Grace thought for a moment then said, 'That's why when I first met my soul family, I thought I saw Ruth Bradshaw who was a terrible bully at school. She used to pinch my lunch and do all sorts of horrible things; I was terrified of her. I was shocked when I saw her but she seemed to disappear and it went out of my mind as soon as I merged with everyone. Surely Ruth can't be part of my family, that would be awful!' she exclaimed.

'It would only be awful if you weren't aware of the bigger picture,' he said. 'Unaware to you, Ruth had been born into a family that were cruel to her. The reason she stole your lunch was because she was hungry and deprived of food. She felt powerless and used you to make her feel powerful, as well as taking food for survival. Her soul created a life that will develop its feelings of compassion and empathy in future lives. In turn, your soul wanted to experience being at the receiving end of cruelty and thus will enhance your empathy and compassion too.'

Grace dwelt on that for a while. 'Oh, that makes me feel dreadful now, if I'd have known that I would have helped her,' she said thoughtfully.

'It wasn't for you to know; it was for you to experience. And remember this is all an illusion, no harm has come to any of you in reality. But you will know this to be true when you have your life review.'

'How do we know what to do or how to behave then to help our soul evolve?' asked Grace.

'When living in the physical we are able to link into the higher-self. The higher-self is the aspect of you in heaven which is able to transmit into the physical and act like a moral compass, which helps us to stay on the right path to achieve the soul's purpose in each lifetime. It is the connection between the soul and the human aspect. The higher-self is housed within the base-self which basically keeps everything together. The soul will also reside within the base-self but essences of it will split off into different lifetimes to then merge back to base when that lifetime is over to add a wealth of experiences and wisdom,' he answered.

'Oh, I see! Is that like when you just have a knowing within you or use your gut instinct? When you know instinctively that you're doing something wrong, even if others try to convince you that it is right?' she added.

'Yes exactly,' he said. 'Sometimes what seems like the wrong path to others is actually the right path for you. The higher-self has all the knowledge you will ever need to access in that lifetime. It knows everything about you, it also knows what your life plan is. When you still your mind and connect to your higher-self all the knowledge is there on tap for you.'

'Why does the mind get in the way all the time, then?' Grace questioned.

'When born into the physical, along with the incarnated soul, we also have an Ego born which will be different in each lifetime. We need the Ego to create an identity for this lifetime, to decide what your beliefs and preferences are, for example what food you like to eat, what your favourite colours are, etc. It will also teach you how to behave depending on the environment and circumstances of your upbringing etc. There are lots of things to consider here. The Ego, however, will try to convince you that 'it' is you. This is not true. Part of the evolution process is to transcend the Ego and connect with the soul to help you discover and remember your true-self and achieve the grandest versions of yourself in that lifetime. You know the Ego is not you because you can watch the Ego and become the observer, see it for all its faults. If you learn to ignore the Ego and see it for what it is then you can access the higher-self and transcend to the soul. The Ego is like having an annoying flatmate that hangs around telling you what to think and how to do things.'

Grace interrupted, 'How do you know, though, if it's the higher-self or the Ego talking to you?'

'Well, that is easy, blessed one. If the advice is generated from love and purity then it's the higher-self, if it's negative then it's the Ego talking,' he answered.

'It's a bit like the devil and the angel sitting on either

shoulder, then, isn't it?' she said.

'Yes, that's a useful analogy,' he replied.

He continued on. 'The soul is attached by a silver chord when you are born onto the Earth. When the silver chord is broken, that is when your time on Earth has ended for this lifetime.'

'What about the spirit? Where does that reside?'

'The spirit is never incarnated on the Earth as it is too pure. The spirit is the life force energy that transcends everything, as it must, because ultimately it is 'All That Is'. The reality is, there is nothing else but pure consciousness, pure joy and unconditional love. And now 'All That Is' is able to experience that love and joy over and over again through the lives that we create and live, watching us evolve back to the highest realms bringing that love, blissfulness and joy back home.'

He turned to move towards the great building. 'Soon it will be time for you to merge back into your base-self and add another layer of this lifetime to your soul. It will be the most incredible, exhilarating experience you can ever imagine possible. There will be much excitement within your soul family as they will all increase their vibrations a little too, as you will all move up the ladder of evolution. Your aura will shine that little bit brighter and the flecks of gold will increase,' he said.

'Is it possible to see where we are in the process of evolution by looking at the brightness of our auras?' Grace asked inquisitively.

'Yes, beloved one, this is true. When you have merged you will understand the level everyone is vibrating at. But there is no one better than anyone else here. We are all from the same source. Some journeys may take longer than others but there is no time here, no hurry and no judgements. We are all just enjoying the same blissful journey of experiencing the illusion of separation to remember and rediscover oneself to then return once more to 'All That Is'.'

Oto paused in front of the building as if he was allowing Grace time to take in the extraordinary energy it was sending out.

'Now, welcome to the halls of healing.' He turned to watch her as she admired the awesomeness of the building. 'Before you merge, I'm going to show you round and take you to a room that I think might interest you.' He started to make his way up the marble steps and Grace followed. Once inside the building, Grace stopped to look around. Although on the outside the walls were shimmering with changing colours, inside the building the walls were all white. As she looked up through the magnificent dome, golden light was shining down into the enormous entrance hall, bouncing off the white walls and shimmering back into the room. The floor was also white and looked as if it was made of marble. She noticed there were lots of spirits moving around, most of them in their spirit form but a few were still in their human form like Grace was.

'What are they all doing?' asked Grace.

'They are working, everyone here has work to do. Some of the work is teaching and some of the work is healing. Think of all the people that have returned home, like you have Grace, and need to merge back with themselves or have some healing. Some of us are working with our mentors, a bit like being back in school,' he replied.

'What are they being taught?' she said.

'It's not like being in school on Earth when you're learning your maths and English, it's more like spending time with a spiritual guru on Earth. Someone who can help you process certain experiences. Help you understand things on a deeper level. Maybe teach you how to connect with your loved ones on Earth to become a spiritual guide or learn how to connect with a healer on Earth to give spiritual healing'.

'I've had some healing, it was amazing. Such a strange sensation,' she added.

'Yes, I know you have which is why I thought this room may interest you,' he said as they moved through the massive entrance hall down a corridor with many doors. After moving passed several doors, he finally stopped at a doorway with a large wooden door. 'Here we are,' he said, as he moved straight through the door without opening it. Grace followed him and found herself inside a massive white room with no floor. In the middle of the room, Grace could only describe what looked like a hologram of a person laying on a bed with a lady standing at the person's head resting her hands on their head. Surrounding the hologram were many spirits all in human form. One looked like a Native American, dressed in his traditional costume. He looked very imposing and was standing slightly away from the person on the bed. There was a small Japanese lady at the foot of the person on the bed also dressed in traditional costume. She had a very pleasant-looking face, she looked calm and serene. There were four men in white robes, two either side standing at the trunk of the person. Then at the head of the person behind the human lady in the hologram stood an attractive-looking Egyptian lady, also in traditional costume with a golden headband decorated with a cobra on the front. She was resting her hands on the lady's head who in turn had her hands on the person laying down. If she didn't know any better, it looked to Grace as if she had just walked in on a strange fancy dress party. The Egyptian lady turned and smiled warmly at Oto.

'Greetings Oto,' she said using telepathy. 'I see you have come to join us. Welcome,' she said, looking at Grace.

'Hello,' Grace replied.

'Greetings Sia,' said Oto. 'Yes, we have come to watch one of your healing sessions. As you know, Grace received one of these sessions on the Earth plain and I thought it might be prudent to let her see a healing session in practice.'

'Of course. I remember it well. Yes. That is a good idea Oto, it is our pleasure to welcome you Grace,' she said, as she continued on with her hands gently resting on the lady's shoulders.

'Come closer, Grace,' said Oto. 'You will see we have the essence here of a person on Earth receiving healing. As you have probably worked out, the lady standing is the healer on the Earth plain,' he said. He then pointed to the Egyptian lady. 'Sia is the spirit leading the healing session. She is being assisted by Ina who is at the feet.' He turned to the Japanese lady. 'These spirits,' he pointed to the men in robes, 'are trainees, they have not long merged with their base-selves and are wanting to explore healing so they can assist the raising of vibrations on Earth.' Oto turned to look at her. 'You are wondering about Ese and his role?' he said, already prompting her next question.

'Yes,' she said, looking over at the Native American. 'I notice he is not standing as close to the patient.'

'That is because he is not involved in the actual healing. He is the patient's gatekeeper. Throughout this person's current lifetime, he will act as their guard or protector. He will make sure that anyone who tries to connect with this person, does so with the purest intentions. He will also make sure that they are able to receive these higher vibrations without becoming overwhelmed. A bit like if you were trying to use a three-amp socket with a 13-amp plug! The gatekeeper's job is to make sure no harm comes to the person, unless of course they choose free will and allow it to happen.' he added.

'Does everyone have a gatekeeper?' she asked curiously.

'Yes,' replied Oto. 'You will meet your gatekeeper when you merge.'

'How exciting!' she remarked. 'How can anything bad happen to them in heaven, though?' she said.

'Remember, beloved one, they are not in heaven, they are still on the Earth realm where we have duality. As you know, all that exists is unconditional love from the purest and highest vibration the 'All That Is'. On the Earth, however, duality was created which means there are lower energies operating on a darker level that could enter their being. Although it can do them no harm here, on the Earth it could make them feel very low and depressed which is not what we are trying to achieve here with the healing. The gatekeeper will ensure that nothing but love and light gets through to them while they are receiving healing.'

'That would be awful if that happened,' she said.

'Take a closer look and see how the healing is going into the person's energy field,' he directed.

Grace looked closer and was amazed to see ten large whirlpools of energy floating above the body in a straight line, as well as smaller whirlpools in different parts of the body like the hands and feet. Each of the larger whirlpools were a different colour and she noticed different symbols appearing over each one. 'Are those the chakras?' she asked.

'Well done, you know your stuff,' he replied.

'Well not really, when I had some healing, the lady kept going on about the chakras and how some of them get blocked. So I just took a wild guess that these were the chakras.'

'Well, you are quite correct. There are ten main chakras as you can see. Now take a look at the one in the middle, just above the naval. Can you see it bends a bit and is spinning at a much slower pace?' Oto said, turning to Grace.

'Yes, I can,' she said excitedly.

'Watch what the healer does now,' he said.

As Grace turned to look, she could see the Egyptian lady directing one of the healers in the robes. He placed his hands over the bent whirlpool and she saw an energy of pure white light leave his hands and move into the whirlpool. As he manipulated his hands, the whirlpool started to straighten up and spin at a greater speed. It reminded her of watching someone on a potter's wheel make a vase out of the whirlpool of clay.

'Why do the whirlpools get so clogged and bent and why does it matter so much?' she asked.

'When you are on the Earth you are not just human you are also beings of energy. The chakras allow the life-force energy that is needed to keep you alive, to travel around the body. Each chakra has a purpose and operates on completely different vibrations to one another. For example, the root chakra at the base of the spine is of a lower vibration closest to the Earth which works more on the physical, the immune system and the fight-or-flight activation. It is very much based on the primal, survival mode, whereas the crown chakra and above operate on a very high vibration and connect you to the spirit realm. On the Earth plain, healers talk about the seven main chakras but there are actually ten main chakras and many minor chakras. People tend not to realise there is the chakra at the feet and two other chakras above the crown chakra. But that is to learn later, beloved one, if you choose to explore healing further.' He took a pause then continued. 'Living in the physical is a much denser and harsher vibration than you are used to and can cause the chakras to clog up quite dramatically. When there is a disease of the flow of energy, the body starts to malfunction and then you can become ill. Things like environmental pollution, the processed foods that you eat, the chemicals that you put in your body like smoking, drugs and alcohol, can all contribute to the chakras clogging. Stress also plays a big part in clogging up the chakras. All of these things can cause harm to the body and then when people get sick, they can't understand why it has happened to them and start to blame it on other things. The human body, when operating properly, is able to cure itself of anything if it wants to. The human body can live to a much greater age than it does at the moment. Remember, you have free will and are able to abuse or not abuse your body if you want to. Most people sleepwalk through life, not listening to their higher-selves or their gut instinct, and then find themselves in a very low place indeed. Sometimes it is part of their life plan to be in this low place but sometimes it is not. If people can learn to raise their vibrations to get the energy flowing around their body as it should, there would be a lot less illness in the world. The sacred breath also has many healing powers. Already on Earth there has been a breathing technique which has been tested by scientists and proved to strengthen the immune system and ward off illnesses, but still, it does not get recognition from the powers that be. There are many very powerful breathing techniques out there for people to try that will do far better than the drugs given at the moment that have terrible side effects.'

Silence hung between them as Grace continued to watch the healing take place in front of her.

Eventually, Grace broke the silence. 'That makes me sad. Isn't there anything we can do to help people on Earth realise this?' she asked.

'Of course. At the moment there are many healers and light workers being born onto the Earth plain. They have lived many, many lives and have reached a high level of evolution and have volunteered to come back to the Earth with one purpose, to raise the vibration of the planet,' Oto replied.

'So, they can change everyone's vibration around them?' she said.

'Not quite. They are not here to change anyone, only one person can do that and that is the person themself, it is not for anyone to change anyone else. The light workers are here to raise their own vibration on Earth, which in turn will raise the vibration of the planet. They are on the Earth to show people the way, like nature shows people the way. Humans forget that they are nature and can live in perfect balance and harmony with the planet. There is enough food and water for everyone. The 'All That Is' has given us this wonderful planet full of resources to live on and experience and create anything we choose. But the 'All That Is' also granted us free will and instead humans have decided to abuse the planet with their misplaced power and greed. People are waking up to this, however, with the help of light workers being incarnated onto the Earth. They lead by example, you will find they are inspirational, motivated and open minded; when people are around them, they feel good about themselves, they feel the positive energies emitting from them. People will naturally be drawn to them and learn from them. But you will notice that they will not preach or try to force or change anyone. For when you use force you are naturally met with resistance – it is one of the laws of the universe. If you push someone they will push back. People cannot be changed or manipulated they can only change by their own free will. If they choose to stay in a dark place, it is their right to be there and their free will. If they choose to change, then there are healers and light workers to lead the way. Humans must also allow each other to be. From a very young age, humans try and manipulate their children to fit into the box that society sets them. Humans concentrate so much on exams and grades that they forget to allow their children to be free and learn in their own way. Children need to be able to explore, be allowed to make mistakes and to spend time out in nature. Children are no longer grounded because they spend hours cooped up inside, they no longer spend time barefoot outside connected to the Earth. The Earth is a wonderful resource with beautiful healing energies which can balance and strengthen your immune system. Humans have forgotten how to be. But light workers can show them the way,' he replied.

'How do you know if people are light workers or not?' Grace asked.

'Think about the people that were around you on Earth, then reflect on what I have just told you. Can you think of someone who may fall into this category that you know quite well?' he asked.

Grace thought for a moment, then love filled her heart as she thought of someone very close to her. 'My god-daughter, Ann,' she replied.

'Yes, well done. Ann is one of life's light workers who has chosen to be born onto the Earth to help raise its vibration and there are many more like her. What would you say is different about her to maybe other people that you know?'

'Well, she is very gentle, kind and humble. She is always looking at being a better person. She will often reflect on situations and think how she could have done something differently. She is also very forgiving and does not judge people, even though sometimes people have not dealt her a very good hand,' she reflected. 'You're right though she doesn't preach to people either, she accepts people for who they are. Some people who claim to be do-gooders just seem to tell you how bad you are and how you must do things their way or suffer the consequences,' she said thoughtfully.

'The golden rule is if someone makes you feel good about yourself, then it comes from a good place; if someone makes you feel bad about yourself, then it is their own inadequacies projecting onto you. You don't need anyone else telling you what to do, you only ever need to go within and tap into the beautiful resources you have always had,' he added.

Grace felt her energy expanding as she thought of her beloved god-daughter. She knew she was a special girl and was glad that she had come into her life as she was a joy to know. They had always got on well and Ann would often come round to visit her, especially after John died. They would spend time talking about spirituality or the different spiritual courses she was doing at the time. She was the same age as her granddaughters and they all got on really well. Her parents were neighbours of theirs for many years and Grace was overwhelmed to be asked to be Ann's god-daughter. She thought that she may be considered too old for the job, but Tom and Claire, Ann's parents were having none of it and insisted that Grace should be her godmother. Of course, Grace was secretly delighted.

She continued to watch the healing session, fascinated by the energy being manipulated and channelled by Sia into the healer on Earth. As well as seeing the energy going directly into the person's energy field from the healers surrounding the person.

She thought back to when she had gone for some healing. She had slight back pain from doing too much weeding, with that and having a healthy dose of curiosity she went to see a healer. Her friend Jenny had recommended the lady. It was back in the seventies when healing was seen as very New Age. She remembered the lady well; her name was Faith. She opened the door in a rainbow-coloured kaftan and led her through to her treatment room, which was very dark and dimly lit. She had incense burning as well as a few candles. Grace felt very relaxed and calm in there. It certainly cured her back pain and she never really had the need to go back for some more healing. She remembered when she was having the healing how strange it felt with the sensation of different hands all over the body at the same time. She was sure the lady healing her had her hands on her head but when she opened her eyes the lady was down at her feet. It was very strange. When she told her experience to others, they just looked at her embarrassed; she could tell they thought she was bonkers, but she really felt other hands upon her at the time and now she knows that was true. It wasn't creepy or anything, it felt great experiencing the waves of energy going up and down her body, with lots of tingling and popping sensations happening. Witnessing the healing taking place from the other side was unbelievable. She wished Faith could see this, or maybe she could, she thought.

'Does the healer see any of this?' she asked.

'Sometimes they do, which is why the spirits tend to stay in their human form, but sometimes they don't. They may just have a feeling or a knowing that their guides are around them. Sometimes really good healers feel that they aren't doing it properly as they can't see or hear their guides and they stop healing, but that really isn't the case. You do not need to see or feel them for it to work, as long as you can feel the energies being channelled or the patient feels it, you know it is happening. They just need to have faith. On the Earth realm it is difficult for humans to trust the un-seeable. Everyone likes to have evidence or be able to see something with their own eyes. They have forgotten to use all the senses that they are born with. For remember, they cannot see the air that they breathe but they do not question that there is air around them, it is a knowing within them. People need to find their faith and trust in their knowing, for it is within their knowing that they must venture to unlock the secrets of life,' he replied.

They remained silent while continuing to watch the healing taking place. Grace noticed that another spirit had entered the room. This spirit was in human form and was standing at the left shoulder of the human receiving the healing, lovingly smiling down at the person. She could see it was a lady dressed in clothes that would fit in well in the sixties. She had a short mini skirt and a beehive hairstyle.

'Who is that?' Grace asked inquisitively.

'That is the recipient's mother. She has recently passed and is taking the opportunity to connect with her daughter,' he replied.

'She looks like she may have died quite a while ago, maybe in the sixties at least judging by her outfit,' she said.

Oto laughed. 'Remember we don't judge,' he said gently. 'The reason the lady is dressed in an outfit from that decade is spirits like to show themselves when they were at their best, or happiest. This would be when the lady felt at her peak. That's why you can't always tell a person's age when they died by looking at them,' he paused, then continued. 'In healing sessions, it is quite common for a loved one to turn up. It is a wonderful thing and the boost of love will only help to raise the vibration of the patient and therefore assist better with the healing. The patient will feel close to the loved one or will have a memory of them whilst the healing is taking place.'

'Oh, how lovely! What a beautiful connection to watch,' she replied, feeling her energies expand out with joy.

'Precisely, beloved one,' he said, as he continued to watch with interest.

Finally, Oto turned to Grace and she felt it was time to move on as he confirmed with his words, 'Beloved one, let us move on. We must make our way to your base-self for the merging to take place. The healing has almost come to an end.' He then turned to the rest of the room. 'Blessings, beloved ones, sending love and light to you all, now we must make our departure but thank you for allowing us to watch the healing.'

The healers all bowed their heads. 'Love and light to you both, too! It is our pleasure and we hope to see you soon, Grace, after your merging,' said Sia.

'Thank you, I very much look forward to it,' Grace said and she really meant it.

Chapter 5

Past Life – Ayyah

As Oto moved back through the large wooden door, they found themselves once more in the long corridor, with the brilliant white light bouncing and reflecting off the walls guiding their path. They continued on for some time, until they reached a huge doorway made of glass or ice; Grace wasn't sure which.

'Is that glass?' Grace inquired.

'No, it is clear quartz crystal,' he replied. 'Clear quartz amplifies energies and brings balance and harmony all around,' he said.

'Is this room where the base-self resides?' Grace asked, a little nervously.

'Yes it is, blessed one, although this is no room,' replied Oto. 'This is a direct link to 'All That Is', where every dimension that ever existed is housed. Beyond this door every soul, every thought, every deed, every possibility of our yesterdays, todays and tomorrows resides. This is the place that connects every single one of us together in a finely woven web of interactions, possibilities and endless creations. Where we all move together, like the oceans and waves forever changing, forever moving. The same waters, the same waves, the same tidal surge, mixing and blending together for eternity, blessing each and every one of us with limitless potential to rediscover ourselves, to reach the highest and best versions of ourselves, that we can become.'

They paused together, preparing themselves for the next step, then Oto instructed Grace to follow him once more, as he moved straight through the doorway without opening it.

Grace followed him with trepidation. Once inside, she found herself floating alongside Oto in a golden light. All she could see was gold surrounding her. Her being started to expand out and rise up, as did Oto's. She could hear and feel an 'AUM' sound vibrating throughout her being; it was deep and powerful but so calming and soothing; it felt wonderful.

'What's happened Oto, where are we? And what is that noise?' she asked.

'Beloved one, that is the sound of 'All That Is'; we are bathing in the wonderful energies. Do not be alarmed blessed one, your soul is calling for you. We are rising to meet with it. All is as it should be, just relax back and enjoy the experience. Your soul essence knows exactly what to do and where to find its home. For this is a powerful and magical reunion. Feel yourself being pulled towards it, where your soul resides. You will feel so whole and enriched,' he said, gently.

Grace wasn't alarmed, she was ecstatic. She was feeling so blissfully happy that joy was rippling throughout her being. With every 'AUM' sound she felt a pull on her silver chord, pulling her upwards; raising her vibration and stretching out her being. The excitement coursing through her body was palpable. The closer she got to her soul, the more the feelings intensified. There was no way of stopping this powerful pull, even if she wanted to. Finally, the vibrations all around her almost exploded and she felt herself burst into a million pieces scattering out everywhere like a shooting star, fizzing across the sky. She then felt herself being engulfed and absorbed by an enormous bubble of energy. She found herself free-falling in slow motion, as an explosion of colour was going off all around her. Her mind started to drift off, as if it was being released from her and all thought was being banished from her mind.

I'm falling, drifting in the delightful nothingness. I feel love cushioning all around me as I float in this blissful joy. My mind is empty of thought, but filled with the loving energy of the universe. There is no sense of time, only complete oneness with 'All That Is'. I feel safe and protected. I completely surrender to this state of ecstasy. As I do so, a haze starts to descend around me whilst images start to come into my being. Faces start to filter in and out of my energy field. I feel an instant surge of connection to them, and crave their energies; willing them into my consciousness until one of the images settles and things start to become clearer.

I'm frightened. I find myself in a hot climate, I know it to be Africa. Terror is gripping at my heart. I know myself to be male and of black origin, and my name is Ayyah. I have a chain tied around my neck and my hands and feet are bound with rope. My body is battered and bruised with whip lashes all over it bleeding and weeping. I'm squashed with other male members of my tribe in a small pen, guarded by men with pale skin holding long metals sticks that have fire and explosions coming from them. Screams are deafening my ears as women and children cry out in sheer terror. I know I have failed my people for I am a warrior, a protector of the tribe. My spirit is weak and the fire in my belly is low. These men come with their fire sticks and kill many members of the tribe; our spears are useless against these weapons. They are taking our women and children, laughing at them and treating them like animals. I pray to Allah for help, I am beyond fury now, fear is a constant companion as I desperately search around from my limited view, looking for my wife and baby son. Please keep them safe Allah, I know I have failed the tribe but the devil has come in the form of man and we need you Allah to protect us from him.

One of the pale faces come into the pen and indicate for us to move, by pushing the metal stick into our backs. The man is ugly, with a long scar going across his face from his *left ear down to the corner of his mouth. His eyes are blue, but dark in colour and menacing. His skin is pink and pale looking, in comparison to my dark, ebony skin. A wildness seeps from his body as he smirks, enjoying wielding the power he has within his grasp. Sweat pours down his face as the excitement builds within him every time he pushes and shouts at us. They wear odd clothes, covering most of their bodies, and speak a strange language. We find ourselves moving in a uniformed line, shuffling along as our legs are bound together with a short length of rope in-between the legs. The rope is tearing at our skin as the sun is beating down hard on our bodies. There is no sign of the woman and children, they have been moved somewhere else by other men. Please Allah don't let them die, they are innocent and only live to serve you, please save them…*

My mouth is so dry, my whole body is stinging and aching now, every step I take is agony. Several men have collapsed along the way, only to be kicked or hit until they stand up, or are fired at if they don't and are left for dead. My only thoughts now are of staying alive, putting one foot in front of the other, ignoring the screaming pain of my body, willing me to stop. Eventually we come to a halt as the sun starts to set in the sky. I look around at the beautiful sunset in this magical land only to see dirt, and shame, like the earth has been violated all around us. We are given a small amount of water to drink and some yams to eat. We scramble about as we all snatch at the water, gulping it down and shoving the food in our mouths before it is taken away from us. There is no conversation between us, as we sit side by side exhausted and broken. Our strong muscles and lithe bodies are no match for their weapons. We know we are defeated and sit silently contemplating our immediate future and that of our loved ones. My thoughts turn to Mairam my wife, and baby son. I wonder where she is now and what's happening to her; I know she will be scared and will be looking for me. The pain of not knowing is greater than the pains from my body. Allah, have I dishonoured you? Are you cross with me? Please tell me what I need to do? I will gladly sacrifice my life for that of my wife and baby son. Why have you unleashed the devil upon us?

Exhaustion has overcome me and I realise I must have drifted off to sleep at some point in the night. The sunlight filters into my eyes as the heat from the sun starts to warm the coldness of my skin, exposed to the night air. I pick myself up from resting on my neighbour's shoulder, as I realise I have been leaning upon him, as he has upon his neighbour. My muscles are starting to cramp and go into spasms from the lack of movement and resting in one position for too long. As I come round, I realise the horror of the predicament I am in. I try to summon up enough strength to make a stand when one of the men comes near, but I am too weak. I look at my once shiny black skin looking dull and savaged with weeping wounds all over my body. A sense of dread washes over me as I realise that Allah has not come. I only hope my wife and son have a quick death and are not played with by these devils in disguise. The man with the scar starts to shout at us, waving his firing stick. He beckons us to stand up ready to move on. It takes a little while for everyone in the chain of ropes to find their balance and get moving again. Another man approaches with a whip and starts lashing out at those of us who are slowing down the procession. I stare at him, I see this makes him feel uncomfortable as he lowers his eyes, I see how weak and feeble he looks. Without his whip or firing stick he would not stand a chance against any of us. He looks very young, no more than a boy; he is thin and short in stature. He looks weak, uncomfortable using this excess of violence. I think he must be around 14 or 15 and must have recently become a man.

I think back to the days of my initiation, before I came a man, when I was called into the bush; where I spent several weeks being initiated. I was excited and proud to become a man. I remember the Kankurang coming to take us to the bush, hiding his face with a mask and his body with bark and leaves. I knew he was protecting us from the evil spirits with his machete. We were a group of five boys all entering the phase of manhood. I was not prepared for the pain of the circumcision; I flinch at the thought of it. I wonder if this man still bears the scar and pain from his circumcision. I knew I had to stay strong to become a man. I remember how all of us went into the bush with excitement and eagerness. I wonder if we would have felt quite so excited if we knew what was about to happen.

However, we quickly learned that pain is important for the journey to becoming a man, you need to be strong to be a warrior; after our time in the bush, pain becomes our friend, something we all learned to cope with. Although I was in discomfort, I still remember the pride I felt being taught the ways of the man, the secrets that had been taught to every man-child over generations. The medicines of the bush, to help with illness and wounds. How to fight and protect and become a good husband and father. How to have many healthy children. I was recently married and had my first-born child, a son. I feel virile and strong producing a son for our tribe, to continue on our heritage. I look forward to having a long line of daughters to help take care of me and Mairam when we are older. I want more sons to contribute to our tribe, and ensure its survival in years to come. What will become of our village and our sacred ways now? The thought leaves me feeling desolate and weary.

We trudge on, the heat is now starting to intensify, and the pale men with their fully clothed bodies are starting to sweat and tire in the blistering heat. Their pale skins are turning pink from the sun. They tease us by drinking vast amounts of water in front of us, laughing. But they do not realise that we are used to the heat and thirst, and can last quite a while without water. Eventually we stop; mainly because the pale men are tired. They bring around some water and a small amount of food for us. We all wearily accept it and drink and eat as much as we are given. We are following the river along to the great waters. My mind starts to race into overdrive as I wonder what their intentions are for us. I know they don't want us dead, as they could have killed us back at the village. Or are we to be sacrificed to their gods, for their victory over our land. I stop praying to Allah as he is not answering my prayers. I wonder if their gods are more powerful than Allah, is that why he has not come? We continue on for several more hours, until eventually we stop for the night. The temperature is getting cooler the nearer we get to the great waters. I have visited the great waters once in a hunting party. I will never forget the sight of the great waters. We were told not to drink the water, as it is full of salt and would make us sick. Great crashes of rolling waves could be seen coming into shore. I had never seen such a powerful display of energy as I did in those waves. I knew that some of the tribes near to the great waters would go out on boats and catch fish from it. Sometimes our tribe would go to the river and catch fish, but this was still a day or so from our village. The great waters were many days away and was too far to travel from our village, except that one time I went. But that visit was more like a rite of passage, for every man has to see the great waters once in his lifetime. To get there we will be passing other villages and crossing their lands. Although they are not hostile, it is still an unwritten law not to hunt in each other's territories. I realise that we have not seen any other tribes on our journey, and wonder whether the pale men have captured any of these tribes.

We settle down for another night; my body is beyond exhaustion. I can smell my wounds now and know they need bush medicine, but this will not be possible. I feel hunger pains rumbling and burning my stomach and try and channel the pain for strength to stay alert to keep my mind working, so I can try and escape and overpower these devils disguised as men. I watch the group of pale-faced men as they start to make a fire. They are sitting round the fire laughing with each other and drinking a potent mixture; I know it is strong as I see it changes them. Their laughter is starting to turn to anger, as some of them push at each other and start to grapple. The man-child sits away from the group looking scared. I can see he is trying to hide in the darkness, hiding from his tormentors. One of the men stands up and takes a while to find his balance, he calls out to the man-child and starts to stagger over to him. He points to us and starts shouting at him, then roughly pushes him over to us. I think he is telling the man-child to watch us while they drink. The man-child comes over to us and uses the whip to hit us, but without much force. This seems to keep the other man happy and he staggers back to the circle around the fire, drinking more of the potent mixture. I wonder if this is a ritual to connect with the devil or their god, but my instincts tell me it is more like a way for them to let off steam. The man-child moves away from us and settles down to sit on a rock.

As night-time marches on, a blanket of sleep overcomes the pale-skinned men. The man-child starts to doze and the camp becomes eerily quiet. All I can hear is the distant chorus of hyenas, laughing in the darkness. Almost mocking us at the situation we are in. I start to drift off, thinking of past memories, happier times. I think back to the birth of my son. How proud I was seeing Mairam holding him in her arms, how strong and healthy he looked. Mairam was radiant, she had never looked more beautiful. I remember when we first met, the shy glances she would show me, seducing me with her eyes. How my stomach did little flips whenever I saw her. How nervous I was when I sent a kola nut to her family as a declaration of my proposal to marriage, and how happy I was when I knew this had been accepted. I realised how perfect our lives were. How simple life had been, we all had enough to eat and drink. We all knew what was expected of us, we followed our traditions and had love and respect for our community. Now all of this had been taken from us in one short afternoon.

I remembered the fierce heat of the afternoon, most of us were resting in the shadows of our huts. The women and children were sleeping, and the men were sitting, reflecting on the morning's work or thinking about their early evening duties when out of nowhere they came. There must have been at least eight pale-skinned men who came charging through our small village firing their sticks. At first, I didn't realise the power of these weapons until I saw Okyebo, my neighbour, fall down in front of me, dead with blood pouring out of his lifeless body. Our tribe had heard rumours of men from other tribes disappearing on their hunting trips, there were whispers that they had been taken by strange men from another land, but our tribe hadn't taken them seriously. I for one certainly hadn't; a decision I bitterly regret. If only we had taken it more seriously, we could have moved the women and children away and maybe set a trap for the pale skins. Now all I could see was chaos and screams of terror, as the men ripped through the village. As the men approached my hut, I knew it was too late to reach for my weapon, so I ran at the men intending to use my fists. This caught them off guard and I managed to hit the first man full in the face, and he went down with a thud. Just as I turned to lunge at a second man, a third man fired his stick at me and I felt something whoosh past my ear. I then felt an excruciating pain as a fourth man started to whip me, like an animal. I reached for him but saw a man raise his fire stick at me and my instincts stopped me, rooting me to the spot as I knew this would kill me. Suddenly I was being pinned down and tied up with rope, and a strange metal collar had been put around my neck. I saw them roughly drag my screaming wife, clutching our baby boy, out of the hut and I then fought like a wild animal to reach her, as they continued to whip me and kick and punch at my body. Eventually I must have passed out, for the next thing I knew I had been tied up with other men from my tribe and kept in a crudely made pen. As I started to come round, I can still remember the shock of seeing what was unfolding before my eyes.

How could this have happened? My senses were being bombarded with noise and smells from the firing sticks and screams from the woman and children. I found it hard to comprehend what I was seeing, as if it was happening in slow motion in a strange dream or nightmare.

Bile started to rise from my stomach as the memories of that terrifying afternoon replayed through my mind. I kept drifting from shock and numbness, to terror of what the future held. Adrenaline was coursing through my body, but I knew my body was too weak to react to the adrenaline, other than by feeling sick and nauseous. I looked around at the state of my fellow tribesmen and knew I could suffer this no longer, I had to do something. My mind started racing, considering different ways I could try and break free. The rope was very strong and the metal around my neck was heavy and weighing me down. My only option was to search for something to cut the rope with, maybe a sharp stone of some sort. I could barely see due to the darkness; the moon was but a slither in the sky. I felt around to try and find something, but it was useless, there was nothing around but dirt and a few small stones. Despair washed over me, my situation was hopeless. I just didn't have the energy to do anything other than breathe.

Time passed on and the sun started to slowly rise in the sky. I could hear the sound of men waking, talking in low rumbles in their strange language. The man-child was awake and sat staring out at the horizon. The man with the scar came over to us and started to shout out strange words. His teeth are black and his face looks puffy and pink. He tips his head back and starts to laugh, placing his firing stick down, then he undoes his clothing and starts to urinate over us. Anger starts to rise in my belly. I wait until he comes closer. I watch him as he picks up his firing stick, then come into the pen to get us to move on again.

A mixture of fear and anger pushes me to reach for his stick as he comes near. The man screams out and hits me hard across the head with the stick. I try to kick out at him whilst lying on the floor, but my legs are restricted with the ropes. I hear a loud explosion go off and a pain hits me hard in the stomach. I look down at my body, as the man kicks me hard in my gut. Blood flows like a river of red from the wound, as my hands instinctively reach down to stop it. The man's face is now close to mine, screaming a stream of words in his strange language, foaming and spitting at the mouth. I start to feel a coldness creeping all over my body. A calmness spreads all around me as his words start to fade in the background. I feel strangely peaceful as darkness starts to seep into my vision until there is nothing but blackness. I find myself drifting, floating in this inky sea, until I found myself falling…

Falling… Falling…

Chapter 6

Past Life – Robert

*A*gain, *as I fall, I start to see faces coming into focus then disappearing back into the fog. Images of places and people ripple through my being as I try to grasp onto them, only for them to float away. I can feel Oto's presence outside of my bubble of energy, gently and lovingly guiding me through my many lifetimes. My being starts to expand as I feel myself growing with layers of energy from different lives encasing me; making me feel whole and complete. I feel an expansion of love and connection occurring, as if I was a tiny piece of a jigsaw now being placed within a picture that is starting to take shape. So many different lives are rushing through me; I can clearly feel whole lives that I've led in an instant, and am able to remember everything about them, especially the impact that they had on me. I concentrate on trying to slow everything down, then I latch on to one of the images and I find myself once more coming to, as the haze that descends all around me starts to clear.*

I find myself in a beautiful drawing room. There is

a raging fire alight in the huge stone fireplace, bringing a warmth into the big airy room. I feel angry. I know myself to be male and of white origin. I feel fat and lethargic, uncomfortable in my own skin. My body feels sweaty and heavy. My name is Robert and I live in England near the coast. I can hear the seagulls squawking in the background, as I look around at my surroundings and know that I have worked hard to achieve such grandeur and splendour in my home. I feel very important, and know myself to be advanced in years. My business is in tin mines and it has been very lucrative over the years. My beloved wife Alice of forty years has died and I know that we were not blessed with children. I have recently married again. My new wife is very plain, and I know I am not in love with her. She is the daughter of the local vicar; she would have easily been left on the shelf to shrivel up and die an old maid if it had not been for me. I married her to produce an heir for me, to carry on my name and continue with the business. However, she is proving to be useless and barren in that department, and now I am left with this albatross around my neck. I am not used to failure; it was difficult the first time when my beloved wife Alice could not produce an heir. But that was different, we were childhood sweethearts and belonged together. Alice is the only person I have ever truly loved. The only reason I married my new wife Agnes was to produce an heir, and without being able to produce an heir, she is no good to me. Just the sight of her repulses me. How she crawls to me begging me to try one more time *for a child; I cannot bear her to touch me now. I have been conned into this marriage, thinking her youth and good health would produce an heir in no time. I have met with my solicitor, for I will not be leaving a penny of my fortune to this fake wife. However, he tells me that will not be easy, as there was no prenuptial agreement signed. I sent him off with a flea in his ear to try and get things sorted. If I have to stay married for the sake of my reputation I will, but I will not be leaving her a penny for her to squander my hard-earned wealth. I shall be leaving it to Alice's niece Edith, a dear child who has always been like a daughter to Alice and I. What a fool I have been! I reach for the whiskey glass and top it up with the finest Scottish whiskey money can buy; whiskey is the only thing that can sooth my nerves since my wife has died. It takes away the pain and dulls the senses, just enough to be able to carry on living in this world without her. Why did Alice have to be taken from me so soon? Why couldn't I have gone first? Alice would be much more equipped to survive in this world without me than I without her.*

As the warmth of the whiskey starts to calm my nerves, I think back to times gone by. My darling Alice is standing there on our wedding day, a vision of pure perfection. Oh, how my heart danced as I saw her coming down the aisle towards me. I had to pinch myself to check that it was real and not a dream. For back in those days I did not have the fortune that I have amassed now. I couldn't believe that a woman as beautiful and intelligent as her could possibly be interested in a man like me, but she was. For forty years she loved me. She was my rock! The reason I have done so well in business I credit to her. She kept me grounded and didn't let me get above myself as I was prone to do. She knew everything about me; all my quirky little ways. She knew about my father, and how cruel he was to me growing up. I flinch at the memory of him; he was a cold, hard man, who would lash out at the slightest thing. He took pleasure in ridiculing me in front of anyone who cared to listen. I was quite poorly as a child and suffered with my chest every winter; I would have to spend days in bed sometimes, unable to breathe properly. He would be furious, as it was one less pair of hands to help, as I was the only son and expected to help with the manual work. I had six sisters and they were all healthy and strong. My dad would often taunt that I should have been the daughter, and my sisters should have been the sons. My mother was terrified of him too. She used to cover for me all the time, doing my jobs when I was too weak, then saying that I had done them. I was always her favourite child, being the only boy; she was a dear woman, so kind and gentle. I was grief-stricken when she died. I was 15 years old and luckily had met Alice by then; she saved me. I shudder to think how I would have coped without her. I moved out immediately after my mother's death; I'd long overstayed my welcome, but didn't want to leave my mother to cope with that brute on her own. By then my health had improved and I was getting stronger and fitter all the time. The rage inside me fuelled my business mind to earn as much money as I could; I worked day and night, and with a good nose for business and with sheer hard work I built up my empire. Unfortunately, my father died before I was able to gloat that his son was not such a waste of space after all. I was determined to make sure that my children never had to suffer at the hands of a brute like my father. But I never got a chance to carry out that promise. My eyes glazed over at the memory of my mother, it was such a long time since I had seen her; her face was such a distant memory. I could barely remember the sound of her voice. How ironic that I could always remember the sound of my father's! I realised it had been a long time since I had thought about my childhood; every waking thought recently had been about my beloved Alice.

Looking back, Alice and I shared such a privileged life together. Our only sadness was the fact we did not have children. It broke my heart to see Alice so distraught at not being able to produce an heir. She felt such a failure. I would always try and lift her spirits and tell her it didn't matter; that she was all that any man could want. But I felt she didn't really believe me, she could read me like a book, I could never tell her that I grieved for our unborn child too; it would have killed her. I would have paid any price to see Alice holding our child in her arms. She would have been such a wonderful mother, she had so much love to give; everyone loved her. My heart is heavy at the tragedy of it all. Not a day goes by that I do not think of my darling Alice.

I feel sick at the thought that I have let her memory down, by marrying too soon after her death. I did not want to be alone, I missed her so much. I thought that I could replace her, or at the very least take comfort in finding company in my latter years. But what a disaster it has turned out to be. I should have listened to Edith, she told me I was grieving and that I shouldn't make any rash decisions by marrying again. I had this notion that I would father a child and the sadness in my heart would be soothed by the love of my new child, even though I did not love my new wife. What a silly fool I am! And now I am stuck with Agnes, and I only have myself to blame. And Agnes of course; my blood starts to boil at the thought of her again. And her stupid father, what a blithering idiot! Call himself a man of the cloth! He had the cheek to insinuate that I was responsible for not being able to father a child! Me! How ridiculous! It was just bad luck that both the women I married were unable to produce children.

I took another glass of whiskey and waited until the smooth golden liquid slid down my throat and started to calm me again. I have a business meeting this afternoon and I need to have my wits about me. I am thinking of buying up another mine in a neighbouring area. It hadn't mined much of late, but I had a gut feeling that they weren't mining in the right area. I knew the owner had hit hard times and I was determined to get a good price for it. I sit pondering for a while on how I will start the meeting. Whether to get straight to the point and make him an offer, or whether to gain his trust and flatter him a bit, then casually make him an offer as an act of kindness, make out I'm not that interested, just doing an old friend a favour to get it off his back. Yes, I think I will go with that tack! I sit back, pleased with myself as I visualise in my head exactly what I'm going to say.

Time for another drink I think, a little reward for being so clever. I pour another whiskey and look at the near empty decanter. I make a mental note to myself to order some more whiskey. It doesn't seem to last as long anymore. When Alice was alive, I hardly ever drank. I used to keep it more to offer people at business meetings. I used to keep their glasses topped up but I would rather have a clear head, so used to barely touch the stuff in my glass. But now it's the only thing that makes my days bearable.

I start to dwell on what action I am going to take with Agnes. It is impossible to have her living in this house with me any longer. It only serves to remind me of how I have tarnished my dear Alice's memory. She will have to go! I start to fantasise about the different ways of getting rid of her. I wonder if I could pay a young man to say that they had been having an affair so I can divorce her immediately in outrage. I chuckle inwardly at the thought. But, no I couldn't do that, she is far too plain! Who would want her! People would know that this wasn't feasible; particularly when she starts to profess her innocence; especially with that father of hers. He is still held in high regard in the community because of his position in the church. I can see him now, defending his daughter in outrage. I think about more extreme measures like getting her pushed over a cliff and falling onto the rocks. I can then feign my grief and show how devastated I am.

No, that was too extreme even for me; I'm not up to getting her murdered. I felt desperation seep into my bones. I could just send her away to the London house maybe; say that she needs to experience a bit of life. Yes, that would be an option. If I was younger, I would pack myself off to London, but that doesn't appeal to me any longer. I can't bear the thought of attending endless, boring parties and having to be polite to people that I can't abide. No, that's definitely not for me. Yes, I've decided, I am going to talk to her wretched father and tell him that Agnes needs to develop a bit more sophistication and experience some life skills in order to become an adequate wife. I'll do that first thing tomorrow, then I'll break the news to her myself. Or maybe write her a letter and go and spend a few days away with Edith and her family. She's always inviting me to come up and spend some time with her. Yes, that's what I'll do, get away for a bit, and spend some quality time with Edith so we can talk about Alice and all our fond memories of her.

I settle back down into my chair, pleased that I have thought of a plan to get Agnes out of the way for a bit. The drink has started to take effect, and I can feel the numbness begin to take over my face and colour my cheeks. It was a comforting feeling, one that I was getting used to now.

Maybe I'll just shut my eyes for a quick catnap. Help me gather my strength for my meetings this afternoon.

A knock at the door interrupts my thoughts. It opens without waiting for a response and Agnes walks in and comes over to greet me. Her face is strained as she approaches nervously in her pathetic timid way. Rage boils up inside me as she dares to come near me to kiss my cheek. I slap her hard across the face and shout at her to go away. It's inconvenient for her to keep interrupting me in her desperate, needy way. I have important things to do, and I can't be responsible for pandering to her needs. She falls to the floor weeping, clutching at her cheek. So weak and silly, Alice would have known not to come into the drawing room during the morning, this is my time to think and get myself together ready for my afternoon business meetings. She almost crawls towards the door and runs out whimpering. I throw my whiskey glass at the door for good measure, just to get the message across that I am furious with her, just in case the slap didn't hit home.

Such a stupid girl, what would Alice think of my vanity, marrying a young foolish girl like Agnes just to prolong my lineage? What does it matter anyway without my beloved Alice. Oh, how I miss you, Alice! Your porcelain skin with your ruby red lips, so full and sweet and tender. I sink back into my chair, exhausted from my outburst. I feel strange as a heat starts to warm up my body from the inside out. Suddenly a pain shoots up my arm and runs into my heart; my breath is taken away from me by the sheer force of the pain. *I try to call out, but I cannot speak. I gasp as I try to fill my lungs with air, but to no avail. For a few short seconds, terror grips at my heart as I process the enormity of the situation. Then just as quickly, I feel a heavy sleep start to descend over me, forcing me to close my eyes, as the last glimmer of light is filtered through them, until I am left totally in the dark. A silence blankets out all sound, and I find myself floating in the darkness. Then I find myself falling into the abyss, free-falling... falling...*

Chapter 7

Past Life – Kareena

I find myself once more drifting into the unknown. Flashes of colours sparkle all around me, as I feel myself expanding out once again; ripples of lifetimes cascading across my being. Such a powerful force of love is encompassing my being, I am connecting up with hundreds of different essences of myself. They are all so familiar now; all the different emotions of hundreds of lives, streaming through my consciousness. Feelings of love, joy, hope, fear, terror, shame, guilt; all the emotions known to man. Memories of loved ones, so much love! Everything becomes transparent as I make connections between characters played out in these lives, to loved ones in my current life. It all seems so natural and perfect. The simplicity of it all is breathtaking; connecting to 'All That Is' brings with it an awareness of the broader realms of existence.

Again, I find the different faces and images start to free flow through my mind. I can't quite hold on to them, until eventually an image starts to settle. I try to slow it down to savour once more the life I have lived.

Once again, the haze starts to clear. I find myself to be hiding in a small dark space. I am a child, and I know myself to be a girl of Indian origin. My name is Kareena and I am seven years old; I'm frightened, I'm hiding from the lady; she is a bad lady. Gita told me if I see her, I must run far away. The lady tries to take us off the streets, but not to a good place. She takes us to work. Gita said she hurts us and maims us so we have to beg for money, then she takes the money from us. Gita said one of the children had her eyes poked out and was left blind; I don't want to be blind; I cover my eyes in terror at the thought of it. The lady is now close to me, but I am small and can hide in very small places. I hold my breath as she walks past me, she does not think to look in the small gap I am hiding in. Gita says I'm smart. She's a good friend; she helps me. Gita is older than me and she knows all the places to go and find food and shelter, as Gita has lived on the streets longer than me. The bad lady is calling out to me, she's telling me that I'm safe and that I can trust her, but I know this to be a lie. I'm hot in this little space; I'm thirsty too, I haven't had anything to eat or drink since early this morning and the sun overhead tells me it's at least midday. When this lady has gone, I will run down to the market to meet with Gita, and we will go and get some food. I am a fast runner and can outrun the old women and men on the market stalls. I'm small so I take the food for Gita and me, as my hands are nimble, I then hand it to Gita as I run past and meet up with her after the chase.

The lady is still there, I cannot see her but I know she is there still. I pray to Vishnu to protect me; I can feel my heart beating loudly in my chest. I wonder if the lady can hear my heart beating. I think of Gita's words telling me to stay put. She told me the lady can smell out fear and that I must remain still for a long time if I'm hiding from her. I try to remain calm; I don't want her smelling me out. I wish Gita was here now, but we got split up running away from her and now I must remain still for a while longer.

I think she may be gone now. It seems like forever I've been stuck in my hiding place. I poke my head out and look around. My eyes take a while to focus as they adjust from the dark. Splashes of colour hurt my eyes from the people's bright clothing and the painted walls. I search but cannot see her. There is mayhem all around me as too many people are moving around in the narrow street, pushing their carts or carrying their wares down to the market. A sacred cow is standing quite near me, chewing on some food that's been left for it, so I stand up and move along behind it, searching round all the time just in case she is here.

After a while I feel more confident that she has gone and start weaving in and out of the crowd, this time looking for Gita. I make my way down to the river where the market is; I usually meet Gita there. I wait patiently for her, eating an orange that I have stolen from a nearby market stall when no one was looking. The sharpness of it makes me shudder as the juice oozes from it, dripping down my already grubby dress. The taste of it instantly transports me back to a time when my mother was alive. We didn't have much but I remember my mother bringing me an orange to eat. The look of happiness on her face as she watches me eating it, laughing at the juice trickling down my face. That was in happier times, before my older brother died. It was just the two of us after my brother died; I never knew my father, and my brother had died after being hit by a train when running across the train track. My mother was inconsolable by his death. I remember watching her for days howling and calling out his name. She didn't stop to eat or drink or even consider me and my needs. It scared me watching my happy mother, who used to dote on me, slowly start to unravel in front of my eyes. I remember trying to make her laugh and even turning her head just so she would look at me. But she just stared back with her vacant eyes filled with sadness. It was never the same after that; she barely managed to work to scrape enough food for us. I never saw my mother eat anything. I just slowly watched her wither away to nothingness. I can hardly remember her face when she was well, like on the day when she gave me that orange. Her shiny black hair and her beautiful brown eyes that would widen when she looked at me. I used to love brushing her hair with my hands; feeling the softness of it under my fingers. Then in return I would get a lovely head massage from her, as she would tell me that it is good for the head and makes your hair grow longer and stronger. I smile inwardly at the memory, but then just as quickly feel the knot in my stomach as I'm cruelly reminded of more uncomfortable memories. Like trying to get the attention of some of the local people that lived near us, willing them to look at us or talk to us so they could see that my mother was not well. Praying that they might intervene and help us; but no one came. I flinch at the last picture I have of my mother in my mind, all skin and bones with sallow cheeks and a paleness that was unnatural. I woke one morning to find her cold as ice with her eyes wide open, staring straight through me. The feeling of fear that gripped at my heart. Not even allowing me the comfort of mourning my mother as I was too preoccupied with my own survival and what would happen to me. I sat for what seemed like days at my mother's side, waiting for someone to come or for my mother to wake up. I knew she wouldn't though, even at that young age I knew she was dead. I prayed so hard to Vishnu and then one time I looked up to see Gita staring at me. She had a beautiful smile, it hit me straight in my heart. The first real show of kindness displayed to me in so long. I didn't want to leave my mother but I knew I could trust Gita, after all Vishnu had sent her in answer to my prayers.

I sit smiling at the memory of Gita, when suddenly my thoughts are rudely interrupted by one of the market stall ladies coming over to shout at me to move on. She says I am putting customers off coming to buy her beautiful materials as I am so grubby. I poke my tongue out at her and move on further up the river, still looking for Gita. It is more crowded up this end; there are people everywhere, all shouting and talking at once. It is harder to find a place to sit and wait in the chaos. I climb up on some empty crates to get a better view and peer over the sea of people, searching out for a familiar face. I marvel to myself at how easy it is to become invisible in a crowd of people, how insignificant Gita and I are. Nobody ever troubles us or checks that we are OK. The only ones to ever trouble us are the bad lady and her people. I got used to people not caring, but as long as Gita and I had each other, that was enough. My heart warmed at the intimacy we shared. Gita was like my mother, father, sister and friend all rolled into one. She was so kind and loving to me; I absolutely adore her.

I hear my name being called but I can't quite work out where the sound is coming from. I turn my head frantically to look. There in the distance I see Gita jumping up and down in the crowd, waving her hands for me to see her. I wave back and wait whilst Gita makes her way towards me through the hustle and bustle. Gita is taller than me but she is older; she is ten years old. She's much thinner than me and has longer hair than I have. One of her front teeth is missing; it got knocked out when she fell out of a building last year when she was being chased, but I think she's beautiful. My heart feels funny at the thought of being together again. I was scared that Gita had been caught! I didn't want to be on my own. I never want to be on my own. It's been two years now since my mother died. If Gita hadn't found me, I don't know what would have become of me. She told me I must leave with her or the bad people would come and find me and snatch me away, as I had no mother or father to protect me; we've been together ever since.

With a squeal of delight from one another, we finally meet up and hug each other hard. Gita tells me she was nearly caught, but managed to kick the bad lady hard in the shins and run off. But she said there are boys working for her now, so we must be really careful in case they find us. We laugh as Gita does an action replay of her kick in the shins to the bad lady. Then we slowly amble along the market searching out where the next food stall is, holding hands, relieved to be in each other's company again. We pass a group of children begging, with bandages wrapped round different parts of their body; we instantly know this signals danger to us. We look around trying to see where the young watchers are; the bad lady places watchers to make sure the children don't run away with the takings. We spot a young boy of about 13 years old sat sleepily on a stack of boxes opposite the child beggars. We quickly change direction and dart back into the crowd to become invisible once more. Gita decides that we need to move away from this area altogether, so we make our way down to the river and retrace our steps, then move in the opposite direction. As we walk, we both start idly chatting about moving out to the country when we are older. Gita says we will marry brothers, and insist that we all live *together in one household. Gita says she wants to have at least seven children. I laugh and agree, but secretly I don't want children or a husband; I just want it to be the two of us forever. It makes me scared to think about getting older and getting married. I feel nervous around men; the thought of marrying feels me with dread. I never knew my father, but I remember snippets about my brother and I have mixed feelings about him. I knew my mother relied on him and he would return with food and money and she would be so happy and proud of him, making a fuss and cooking him nice food. He was 14 years old when he died; he was nine years older than me. So through my mother I used to be happy at his return at the end of the day, but in reality I used to be a bit frightened of him. I knew I irritated him and he would often push me out of the way and be rough with me if I ever got close to him. I don't remember much about him, but I do remember staying out of his way whenever he returned, and letting him have time with my mother on his own. My mother used to encourage this by making me go to sleep early, telling me I needed my rest, but I was never tired and used to lay wide awake listening to the low rumbling sound of their conversation. There was never any love from my brother towards me, only coldness. I feel a sense of shame when I think of the relief I felt when I found out he had died. It was only when I saw the depths of my mother's grief that I knew it was wrong for me to feel this way, and wished he was still alive. I feel strange thinking about my mother and brother, it makes* my tummy feel unsettled. I wake up from my daydreaming and start to chat again to Gita, hoping that she didn't notice I wasn't listening to her.

We continue to walk and find ourselves at the quieter end of the market. There isn't quite the same frenzy of people. It's a much slower pace around here, and I feel myself instinctively taking a deep breath of air, filling my lungs with calmness after leaving the chaos behind. The air smells fresher without the deep heavy scent of spices and food attacking my senses. By now its mid-afternoon and Gita is starting to get hungry, so we search around to see if there is anywhere that has some food, as this is not the area where food is usually sold. We find a street seller who is selling rice and curry. I know this is not the place to steal food from, especially something like curry, so I go up to the seller and hope she takes pity on me while I beg for food. We get lucky – the lady says she has come to the end of a batch and would not be able to sell the scrapings anyway, so, she hands us both some rice and leftover bits of chat sauce which we hungrily eat, stuffing it into our mouths without waiting to swallow. It feels good feeling the emptiness in my tummy start to disappear. The lady smiles at us, then half-heartedly tells us to clear off and not to come crawling back tomorrow thinking she was an easy touch.

We carry on, wandering along the riverbank. Gita says maybe we should stay away from our usual camp under the bridge tonight, just in case the bad lady has got wind of us being there. So, we decide to look for a place to sleep early. The nights are so warm, we don't need to worry about cover from the elements, but we do need to worry about being discovered by the bad lady. There are lots of buildings being built further down the river. Gita suggests they may have somewhere where we can sleep safely, where no one will find us until the morning, so we carry on walking towards the new buildings. As we approach them, we can hear the noise of people banging and crashing with their tools. We hover back a bit from the workmen and look at the different buildings that are going up. We both decide that a building that has a roof on looks the best bet to sleep tonight and we make an agreement to go back later after dark, when the men have gone. We head down to the river to have a drink and cool down. We find a spot with a big rock beside the river where we can sit and dangle our feet in the water. I reach down and cup my hands full of water and take in a quick drink. I know you're not supposed to drink from the river, as it can make you sick, but I'm thirsty and there is no other water around. I like to watch the boats drift up the river; it's nice to sit there listening to the gentle splash of the water lapping at the boats. For once, I don't feel hungry and the sun is now a pleasant heat shining down on my face. We both sit quietly, just enjoying the moment, comfortable in each other's company, watching the sun bouncing off the sparkly water. I start to feel sleepy so I lay back on the rock, resting my head in my hands which are entwined behind my head.

I look up at the endless stretch of blue sky, admiring its beauty. Gita does the same and we lay side by side on the rock, with our feet dangling in the water. My eyelids start to become heavy, and I feel them slowly starting to close like a lead weight. The sound of the water slowly sending me off into a dreamy sleep.

Just as I was about to fall off to sleep Gita wakes me up with a terrifying scream, and she shouts at me to run. I see the bad lady approaching with two boys, who look like they are about 14. They are all calling out to us but we do not wait to hear what they are saying. We both make a run for it, dashing back to the marketplace, trying to lose them, weaving in and out of the market stalls, but the crowds are not so busy here. I follow Gita as best I can, but her legs are longer. She heads further down the riverbank and tries to lose them, jumping on to some boats that are moored there. I follow her, jumping from boat to boat. I can feel the boys start to gain on us; they are calling out to us to stop. I keep going, I can feel my lungs are burning from breathing so hard; adrenaline is coursing through my body with sheer terror. Gita stretches out her long limbs to jump to the next boat, but I know as I jump my legs are not going to reach. Fear almost chokes me as in that split second, I know I'm going to fall in the water, but I cannot swim. I want to call out but there is no time. I hit the water hard and swallow a mouthful of water; I try to kick my legs out to reach the surface, but I feel my body being pulled down. As I find myself under the water, I try to breathe and mouthfuls of water start to fill my lungs. I can't see anything as the water is so dark. I thrash out with my arms and legs for as long as I can. Just as I feel my lungs are going to burst, a calm descends over my body; I no longer feel scared. I find myself surrendering to the water, as I sink down to the bottom of the riverbed. I find myself strangely sleepy, my eyes are closing and I feel safe being cocooned in this darkness. I find myself falling, feeling incredibly light, but falling... falling... falling...

Chapter 8

Past Life – Beth

O nce again, I find myself falling in the abyss, I feel totally at peace and feel the layer of my last life as Kareena start to meld in with my other lives; bringing that beautiful sense of wholeness to my soul. Feeling so much love and connection to Gita and the other cast of characters in my last story told. Seeing the beauty of the tragedy played out by my fictional self Kareena, and feeling all of the love and compassion I have developed and enjoyed in this lifetime, with Gita and my mother. How my fear and terror of the bad lady, and the fear I felt towards my brother, have helped to intensify my feelings of love for Gita and my mother, and my tragic circumstances have helped me to enjoy the beauty and simplicity of nature all around me. I start to see more faces and images fly past me. I try to grasp onto one of the faces but they flick past me like a row of dominoes colliding, tumbling past in a sea of faces. I force myself to lock onto one of the faces, and an image starts to become clear as the haze starts to lift. I feel myself coming into the last of the fog and I know my journey is coming to an end.

As I start to come around from the haze, I open my eyes and find myself in a small dimly lit dwelling. I know myself to be female and of white origin, my name is Beth. I'm helping an elderly gentleman who has ulcers on his legs; I am tending the wound with a mixture from the bowl I am holding. The man is in pain; he winces as I touch his leg. He is telling me that I must be careful not to let anyone know that I am a healer. I listen to him but do not pass comment. I know the man cares for me and is worried that I will be accused of witchcraft. I carry on tending to his wounds until I have finished. The man is a neighbour who has known me for my whole life; he calls me little Beth. He takes my hand and squeezes it in appreciation. I tell him to rest and raise his leg onto a little wooden stool. Although the room is dark, it is warm and cosy; there is a fire burning in the hearth which is just enough to light up most of the room. I make him a drink of nettle tea and bid him farewell as I gather up my things. As I walk back to my home, I reflect upon his words. There has been a lot of unrest in the surrounding villages; apparently a man of standing is coming round and taking any local healers he can find to the castle, and keeping them under lock and key. They are all women of course, and have all been accused of witchcraft and being in cahoots with the devil. The women in my family have been healers for generations, it's what we do. My mother and father have told me that we must keep the healing to just a few trustworthy people for now, until this man disappears. How can anyone mistake healing for making a covenant with the devil, and therefore becoming a heretic to Christianity? Healing is a loving act which comes from the heart and from nature, what has that got to do with the devil? I don't have anything against Christians, but my religion is nature.

There were whispers that these men come with women, who prick the skin of the so-called witch. They believe that the witches bear a witch's mark, which will not bleed or they will feel no pain from it. If they find a mark on your body then they will prick your skin where the mark is, and if it does not bleed this would go towards sealing your fate. Already a few local women who I didn't know, but were from nearby villages, have been condemned to the gallows. I shudder at the mere thought of it. As I reach home, I notice two shiny black horses outside tied up to a nearby tree. I walk up the little path leading to my home and enter through the same little wooden door that I have walked through all of my life. Inside are two men standing next to my mother and father. One of them is obviously a soldier, as he is armed with a weapon. He is short but stocky, and has a serious-looking face. The other man is taller and slimmer, with a thin moustache and a pointy looking beard. I notice his face is also pointy and it reminds me of something feral, like a rat or mouse, and his clothes seem very grand and expensive. The house is small and the place looks very cramped having these extra men inside. It doesn't suit the house; they look totally out of place. The tall man greets me warmly, but I can sense there is a bad undercurrent happening between my parents and the men. I nod but don't respond as I am unsure how to react. He asks me where I have been, and I tell him that I have been round to visit my neighbour. He then asks me what my business was there. I explain that our neighbour is a friend and was feeling unwell, so I had made him some food and something to drink. He looks down at my bag and asks what I am carrying with me. I hesitate then show him my bag containing the empty bowl of the mashed-up mixture. Luckily, I have used up all of the herbs; he asks me what was in the bowl. I look nervously at my parents, then tell him it was a mixture for a stew that I had made him. He comes closer and uses his finger to taste a bit of the mixture. He pulls a face and complains how bitter the mixture is. I tell him that once you've added some stock and potatoes and carrots it tastes a lot better. Silence falls on the household; you can feel the tension hanging in the air as we wait for his response. He remains thoughtful for a moment. He tells me that he has been told that my mother and I are healers and are using witchcraft. My mother pleads ignorance and states categorically that we would never dabble in witchcraft, that it is a sin and that it is a crime against God. As the man continues to stare at us, the tension heightens and my mother moves forward to grab his arm, once more protesting our innocence. My father holds my mother back, as she clings on to the sleeve of the tall man. The soldier reaches for his weapon whilst pushing her away. My father speaks next and vehemently denies that there is any wrongdoing in this house. He is a man of God and would have no witchcraft practised in his house. My stomach starts to churn, as the tall man looks down on my father and sneers at him. He says that if we have nothing to hide, we won't mind if he takes me to the castle for further questioning, just to prove our innocence. He mentions the pricking that will be done to check our claims. My mother shrieks and throws herself down at his knees for his mercy. She begs him to take her instead but he just laughs and says not to worry as he will be back for her in due course. Again, the soldier pushes her away and my father lunges forward to protect her, only to be thrown against a wall. There is a loud thud and he falls limply to the floor. My mother screams and rushes over to him. The tall man then turns round and tells the soldier to take me away. He gathers me up over his shoulder while I scream and thump on his back to put me down. The tall man grabs at my hair and tells me to stop screaming or he will take my mother away too; this silences me quickly. I start to cry as the soldier roughly throws me up onto the horse and speeds off with me, following the tall man's lead. We ride for some time, at least a couple of hours, until we finally reach the castle. It is an enormous, cold-looking, formidable building. Fear is coursing through my veins. As we make our way across the drawbridge, I notice the different people milling around, carrying on about their business. Nobody gives me a second glance as we make our way into the courtyard. The soldier dismounts and drags me off the horse to the floor. He brings me to a stand then roughly pushes me in the back and tells me to get moving. The tall man moves away in a different direction as the soldier and I make our way into the castle from a different entrance. It is cold in the castle; we make our way down a narrow staircase; the air gets colder the further down we go. The narrow corridor is dimly lit and I am taken into a damp room, which is sparsely furnished with a table and two chairs. He orders me to sit down, then leaves the room and shuts the door behind him. I can hear the key turn in the lock and through the few bars that were set into the thick wooden door, I see him walk away.

Panic fills me with fear. What is going to happen to me? Surely, they can't believe that I am a witch. And what has happened to my father? The sound of the thud against the wall as he hits his head is replayed in my mind; I feel nauseous and run to the corner of the room to be sick. My mind is racing with scenarios, none of them good. I have heard such dreadful things about what happens to a convicted witch; I sit shivering, terrified of the outcome. A few minutes pass then the door unlocks and a lady walks in with the tall, thin man. She orders me to undress. I hesitate so she slaps me hard across the face. I wince and immediately start to take off my clothes, trembling, fumbling at my undress. As I stand there naked, she starts to examine every aspect of my body, whilst the tall man watches. She points at a skin tag on my shoulder which I have had for as long as I can remember; she tells him it is the devil's mark. I tell them that she has made a mistake, that the skin tag has been there for years, but they won't listen. She takes out a sharp-looking instrument then prods it into my skin where the skin tag is. I wince again at the pain, then she looks triumphant, as she withdraws the instrument only to show the tall man there is no blood. I don't understand what is happening, how can this be? I start to cry again, pleading for them to listen to reason.

They cruelly exit the room and leave me crying in a ball on the floor. Eventually coldness brings me back to my senses and I pull on my clothes. Nobody comes for me tonight, I am left cold, hungry and thirsty. I lie on the floor overcome by exhaustion. I wonder how my parents are and I know how terrified they will be feeling. I pray that my father is OK after that sickening crack to his head, and I hope if he is OK he won't do anything silly and get himself in trouble over me. My dear mother will be beside herself; she will be praying for my safe release. How will they cope without me, it will destroy them? I spend the rest of the night in torment, imagining the horrible events that await me, replaying them over and over again in my mind. But also worrying about my parents, sickened to the stomach of how distressed they will be. My stomach is churning, burning with hunger and knotted with fear. I feel so cold that my body will hardly move as it is stiffened from lying on the cold, hard floor. I have no idea of time. It is so dark down here, there are no windows. I can hear people shouting and screaming in rooms next to me; I cover my ears, trying to block out the horror of my predicament. I try to think back to happier times to calm my racing mind but it is no good, as my mind betrays me with images of what is going to happen to me.

After the longest night I have ever known, they come for me. Two soldiers enter the room looking mean and menacing. They only speak to tell me to stand up. They tie rope around my wrists and push me forward to walk back along the narrow corridor and up the cold winding stone staircase. When I reach the top, I am moved back towards the entrance I came into last night. Once outside, I pause to adjust my eyesight and take in a deep breath of fresh air; the air is warmer outside than it is down in the castle. Then I am shoved roughly inside a wooden enclosed cart with bars on the doors. I find myself sitting next to a man who smells very strongly of urine; the smell is burning my nose, so I turn my head to breathe in fresher air from another direction. He tries to speak to me, but I keep my head down and don't respond. He then starts to laugh hysterically, before continuing to talk to himself for the rest of the journey. We continue on for a couple of hours as I settle down to the jig of the cart, my body softly bouncing around, soothing my emotions with its repetitive motion, bringing me a small solace of comfort in this desperate hour of need. Finally, we come to a standstill, and I am again roughly deposited out of the truck and onto the ground. Different men come forward and drag me into a large room, which is crowded with lots of people all jeering and screaming. My senses are overloaded and I can't hear what is being said. I can feel the hostility directed at me, but I can't comprehend what is happening. Then a man seated on a stage with a mallet starts banging on the table in front of me, directing words at me. There is a roar in the room as people start to scream at me and throw things. People are spitting in my direction and the two men who brought me into the room roughly manhandle me once again out into a courtyard. The place is packed here too as people start to make their way out of the room with me. I am taken up some wooden steps, then I see the ropes that are hanging down and I realise that I am at the gallows. I scream with sheer terror and feel my bladder and bowels empty as I shake from head to toe. A man of faith comes up to me and starts to talk in a language that I don't understand. I plead with him to help me, he gently touches my shoulder and says a few more words, then turns to walk away. A man then steps forward and places a noose around my neck, then I hear a loud noise and I drop out of the floor.

I gasp then feel myself catapulted into a blackness; I feel strange. All feelings of fear have gone and I am being comforted by this inky blackness that surrounds me.

I feel myself starting to float. Ripples of love start to gently rise and fall all over my being. I feel myself expanding out as the 'AUM' sound starts to vibrate through me once more. How comforting and soothing the vibrations are. I can hear Oto softly in the background providing me with feelings of comfort and encouragement. His presence is felt outside of the bubble that I am in, surrounding me with love. With every face and image that comes into my being, a layer of energy is added to my soul. I feel the intense feelings from every single lifetime. I instinctively know who has played the different characters from my past lives. I know that when I was Ayyah, my wife Mairam was my mother from this lifetime. When I was Robert, my wife Alice was John and my second wife Agnes was my uncle Joe from this lifetime. Gita was Michael and I was shocked to discover that the bad lady was John. When I was little, Beth my mother was James and my father was my sister in this lifetime.

It is a strange mixture of emotions; I bear no ill feelings to my kin who were my enemies in these lives. In fact, I feel nothing but love for them. Grateful that they can love me enough to go through these lives as brutal people, to help me evolve to the highest version of myself that I can become. How none of this is true reality, but a facade to experience different relationships, different emotions, make different choices. How time and time again I can love these people from different perspectives. I feel an overwhelming wash of love and connectedness to them. I can feel myself melded with everyone from my soul family, knowing that in every lifetime we are all connected; even if we aren't incarnated into the same lifetime, there is a connection to them in heaven. I start to feel myself growing in wholeness. Knowing that I am a multi-faceted multidimensional being. It is in this moment that I realise that I was never complete as Grace Sullivan, just a mere essence of my being. In this lifetime, I can see how disconnected I was from my being without even realising it. Merging with my other lives has made me feel so divinely whole. Gloriously restoring me to a higher level of being. I am now aware of the bigger picture. Knowing where I have come from and where I am going. Understanding myself and my kin on such a deeper level. The road has been long and hard, but the rewards when we return once more to heaven are so spectacularly exhilarating and ecstatic. Being reunited with your soul family and 'All That Is' is the most incredible feeling that we will ever experience. Love is such an overused and understated word on the Earth realm. There is no love on Earth that comes even close to the ecstatic love that is experienced in heaven towards the soul family and 'All That Is'.

Chapter 9

Different Lives of Grace

*J*ust when I think that my soul can't expand anymore, I *am stopped in my tracks by a formidable presence that has come into my bubble of energy. It isn't Oto – I can feel he is still outside of my bubble – but this magnificent presence feels very familiar. I find myself instinctively opening up to these pure and powerful energies, greedily absorbing them into my being. I feel the protection and love emanating from them and I find myself willing them to wrap around my being forever. A haze that once again descends all around me starts to clear, and I can feel an image start to come into my awareness. A spirit in human form emerges in front of me. He has the blackest of skin and is wearing a colourful kaftan and an African fez. I know immediately that this man is my gatekeeper. I even know his name is Eli, everything is coming back to me.*

    'Greetings Asa,' he booms in his deep African voice. 'It has been a while since we have spoken.' He pauses, smiling, then continues, 'It has been my greatest pleasure to watch you grow and evolve on the Earth realm, beloved one.'

'Eli!' I shout. 'I didn't realise how much I have missed you! I didn't feel you around me on the Earth realm so much this time,' I reply, feeling so overwhelmed with love by his presence.

'That's because I was not needed so much, you have kept yourself safe and looked after yourself. You have made my job so much easier than lives gone by, I'm pleased to say,' he laughs.

'Yes, although I had a great tragedy in this lifetime, I was able to stay more connected this time, without even realising it. I followed my instincts and listened to my intuition,' I reflect.

'You have remembered well, beloved one,' he says, as we both continue to soak up each other's energies.

We continue in this moment for a while, communicating with one another using our energies; I am not ready to release Eli from my being yet. I am enjoying our reunion, although strictly speaking we have never been apart. How did I not realise on the Earth realm that Eli was with me? It's incredible that I lived my life so blinkered on the Earth. Every time I incarnate, I always feel that I will remember immediately when I am born, that I come from pure energy, as I cannot believe that I would ever forget, but every time I do! I feel as though I have been sleepwalking on the Earth realm.

'Blessed one, you know that the main importance of being born onto the Earth is to drink from the cup of forgetfulness; remembering is the journey, the route to your evolvement. If you know your connection with heaven and 'All That Is' there would be no point in experiencing the Earth plain, would there?' he mocks gently, in his deep rich voice.

'I know! I know!' I exclaim. 'Forgive me,' I laugh. 'I have only just arrived and I'm just taking it all in again; remembering for the countless time, anyone would think that I've never done this before,' I say jokingly.

He laughs with me, then I notice his demeanour becomes more serious. 'Well beloved one, are you ready for your life review now?' he asks.

I know this part is to come and I am looking forward to it. I feel that I have had a long and happy life, although I was blighted with tragedy; I had loving relationships and feel that I have evolved well in this lifetime. However, I also know that I will have glimpses into other lives that I have lived as Grace Sullivan, and wonder what awaits me. 'Yes Eli, I am,' I reply confidently.

'Now just to remind you beloved one, you are still attached to this current life with the silver chord. When you merge with your other lifetimes as Grace Sullivan, it will be as an observer, not the same as it was with your past lives, when you were able to step into those lives and feel as if you were living that life in the present moment.' He waits for a response from me.

'Yes, I remember, I can step into any lifetime I choose as Grace Sullivan, but I cannot change anything, I am just watching,' I say, waiting for confirmation.

'Well, that's not strictly true,' he says. 'You are now connected to your higher-self, so on some levels you can change things, if the Grace Sullivan you are watching is seeking out connection to her higher-self.'

'Yes of course, I understand that,' I say. 'Shall we start?' I say eagerly.

Eli smiles and energy ripples are sent up and down his being in response to my keenness. He then moves in closer to me and very gently says, 'Now beloved one, remember it is your will that takes you to the lifetime that you choose. Bring that lifetime into your awareness, then you will pass through the veil into that dimension.'

I smile as it all comes back into my awareness, then I concentrate on bringing a lifetime I have lived as Grace Sullivan forward. I feel my energy expand as I will it so. A whooshing of energy pulls me through the thin veil, taking me to another time and dimension. As energy starts to settle all around me, I find myself on the physical plain, accustoming to linear time once more.

I find I am in the kitchen of a home I don't recognise. There is washing-up piled high, with dirty dishes on every surface. I can see someone sitting at the kitchen table, a lady, she has her head bent over the table buried in her arms. I can see a mass of dark hair messily tumbling down over her arms; it sounds like the lady is crying. Little sniffs and sobs are being gently let out in-between breaths. I am then distracted by the sound of a baby crying, and follow the direction of the noise into a small sitting room with stuff piled up everywhere. I can see a big Silver Cross pram with little feet kicking up every few seconds in between wailing screams. I look over into the pram and am shocked to discover James staring back at me, with his cute little chubby face which is now bright red from screaming and crying. I'd recognise that adorable little face anywhere. It suddenly registers that the lady at the table must be me. I move back into the kitchen to take another look. By this time, Grace has lifted her head up and is busy wiping her nose. She slowly stands up and makes her way towards the sitting room; she looks tired and worn out. She has dark circles under her eyes, with a tinge of redness around the lids. I feel saddened at her appearance, her hair looks like it hasn't been brushed and her clothes appear crumpled and stained. As she starts to drag herself slowly into the sitting room, she calls out to James in a weary, desperate tone, 'Please James, will you stop crying! What do you want? I've fed you! I've changed you! I can't do this anymore!' I am surprised at the level of desperation in her voice, her aura is dark and muddied all around. I know from this that she is very depressed; something I never experienced in my current lifetime other than with grief. Both my times as a new mother were the happiest I had known in my current lifetime.

I follow her into the room and watch as she goes over to the pram and bends down over James. 'What? What is wrong?' she shouts at James, waiting for a response. James continues to cry and I can see his little body soaking up the darkness being released from Grace's aura. She stops and clutches at the pram and bends her head down. 'Please help me! I can't take any more of this,' she sobs, as a fresh load of tears pour down from her face. I move in closer to try and offer some comfort, by merging my energies with hers. I know I am connected to our higher-self and can access healing for Grace through this process. I expand out my being, and completely encase Grace and James in my energies. As I do this, I feel a strong energy sweep into my awareness, bringing with it such a powerful, loving force. A beautiful, enormous angel starts to materialise, its huge wings unfolded ready to wrap them around our energy, as it steps forward to join me in merging with Grace and James. Golden threads of energy are emitted from this glorious being; weaving into Grace and James's auras. The healing energy being directed from the angel is on such a high vibration, that I automatically find myself responding to it, with a rippling motion being sent out throughout my energy field. I feel Grace start to react to the healing as she yawns, and notice James's wailing is slowly brought down to a slight whimper. 'There, there,' says Grace, as she gently picks James up. 'What's all that fuss for, hey? Are you trying to finish your mummy off?' she says gently, as she starts to rock James back and forth. She makes a gentle shooshing noise and James responds by cooing at her, as his eyes slowly start to close, as if they have lead weights attached to them. I feel the energies around the room change as the darkness starts to dissipate when the light hits it. The beautiful angel remains there for some time, until Grace and James have calmed down. The angel is Grace's guardian angel and is spectacularly beautiful. Every soul's lifetime has one of these magnificent celestial beings assigned to them for unconditional love and protection throughout that lifetime. My awareness reminds me of the times throughout my many lives that I have been helped or saved by these extraordinary beings. Their energies and vibrations are different to ours, they are able to manifest on the physical plain as an intermediary between the 'All That Is' and our lives, as humans on the Earth plain. Another beautiful gift of love sent to us from 'All That Is'.

Grace gently lays baby James down into the pram to sleep and returns to the kitchen. She sighs as she looks around at the mess surrounding her. She notices the clock and sees that it's 4.30 pm, so makes her way over to the sink and starts filling it up with detergent and water. Slowly, she starts to place the plates into the sink and works her way through the mountain of washing-up, stopping every so often to wipe the plates and put them away, before she can move on to another pile of plates, as there is a limited amount of space. As she's nearing the end of the washing-up, a key is placed in the lock and John boisterously barges his way through the door, calling out in a loud voice that he's home. Grace rushes to the hall and places a finger to her mouth, shhshhing him to be quiet. He stops immediately in his tracks, then does an exaggerated tiptoeing into the kitchen, and leans over to give her a kiss. 'How's your day been, darling? How is my favourite little man doing? Has he been behaving himself?' He smiles, then continues speaking before she has a chance to respond. 'I've missed you both so much today!'

Grace slumps herself down at the table. 'I've missed you too John, he won't stop crying! All day! He just screams and screams! I've fed him and changed him, I'm just so tired!'

John's face changes and looks concerned. 'Well, is he OK? He seems to be asleep now.'

'Yes, I know he's asleep now! And so he should be, he's screamed all day! Of course he's alright, he's doing it deliberately, just to spite me, I'm sure of it!' she retorts aggressively.

'Don't be silly darling, he's a baby, of course he's not doing it deliberately! You're just tired. Why don't you go and have a rest, I'm here now, I can take over when he wakes up. Have you remembered to take your tablets and have you eaten anything today?' he asks gently.

'I don't know, I'm too exhausted to think! I need to sleep,' she says, as she stands up and makes her way over to the stairs. Slowly she starts to climb the wooden hill, with heavy laden feet, looking up as if she is about to climb Mount Everest instead of a staircase.

After she has gone, John sits down at the table and takes off his tie and unbuttons his shirt. The strain starts to show on his face and he sits there for a few minutes, taking deep breaths while holding his head in his hands.

He then gets up and makes his way into the sitting room and stares down into the pram. His face lights up as he looks down on James sleeping and gently strokes his cheek. As he does this, his aura starts to expand out and beautiful loving energy gently encompasses James as he sleeps. The deep bond between the two of them is touching to see.

For now, this moment of despair and desperation is averted, but sadly I realise this will not be the case in future times.

As I see the future ahead of me, I know Grace will be blighted in this lifetime with depression. It will affect her relationship with both her sons, and to her husband John. Sadly, for them, their marriage doesn't work out. The relationship between John and the boys will be strong, but the relationship with their mother will be distant. James's relationship to his wife will also be challenging in the future, because of the ramifications of the poor relationship with his mother. But Michael will go the opposite way, he will marry and have a good relationship with his wife, as he is determined that his marriage doesn't turn out like his parents'.

Although I feel saddened at this outcome, I also feel strangely detached from this lifetime. It's like I've been watching a movie, and I'm sad for the characters but I know this is not a true reality. I can see the bigger picture in Grace's evolvement or more accurately my evolvement. It is because of the journey that I endured in this lifetime, that I have received such a loving, rewarding and satisfying role as a mother in my lifetime. I can honour and respect the journey that I had to endure, to reach where I am now. This is where the role of self-love is so important in all my lifetimes.

I settle back to my awareness and start to bring in another lifetime lived as Grace Sullivan. Again, as my being expands and my energies change, I feel a whooshing sensation as I am pulled through the veil into another dimension.

I find myself in a little café, situated in a busy road. I can see the heavy traffic moving past the window. There are several tables and chairs of all different types placed around the room, uniformed with a crisp white tablecloth laid over each of them. There are little vases of flowers on each table, along with a menu and a little salt and pepper pot. The tables are filled with people chatting away, enjoying a cup of tea and a bite to eat. As I look around the room, I spot a familiar face sitting at one of the tables. Grace is sitting there on her own, drinking a cup of tea and reading from a newspaper. She is smartly dressed, wearing a navy skirt and a cream silk blouse and looking very fetching. Her dark hair is smooth and shiny, pinned up at the sides. She is wearing make-up and looks particularly radiant. She looks as if she is in her late twenties, maybe early thirties. The room is noisy from constant chatter, but it doesn't seem to bother Grace as she carries on reading, engrossed in her newspaper. The café door opens and a blast of fresh air enters into the room causing Grace to look up. She looks shocked as her gaze fixes on the gentleman coming into the room; the colour drains from her face and she continues to stare transfixed. I can see the back of the tall man. He has a shock of dark hair and is dressed casually in trousers with a jacket. The waitress makes her way over to him and asks him if he would like a seat. He says that he would like a table for one. As he starts to speak, I recognise his voice and realise that this man is John. The waitress explains that all of the tables are occupied. As she starts to talk, John turns round and surveys the room, looking at the full tables, when suddenly his eyes rest upon Grace.

'Grace? Is that really you?' he says as his face lights up, and he moves over to talk to her.

'John! My goodness! I can't believe it's you after all this time!'

The waitress moves in closer, waiting for an instruction as to what he wants to do.

'Are you sitting on your own?'

'Yes, I am, would you like to join me?' she asks, excitedly.

'I'd love to,' he says as he takes off his jacket and starts to sit down.

'What would you like to drink?' the waitress asks.

'Erm, can I have a pot of tea, please? Grace, would you like another cup?'

'Yes please,' she replies.

John turns to the waitress. 'Make that two pots please.' The waitress smiles and walks away as John turns to look at Grace.

'Grace, you look amazing! You haven't aged a day since I last saw you!' He stopped and flinched at that comment and an awkwardness descended upon them. Grace looked uncomfortable then nervously started to talk.

'You look marvellous yourself, how have you been? What brings you to London?'

'Well, I've lived here for ten years now. After you decided not to come with me, I thought I've got nothing left to lose, so I came anyway and found a room to rent, then a job at a small accounting firm and I've been there ever since.'

Grace almost choked on her drink. 'Sorry, did you say when I decided not to come to London?'

'Well… yes,' he answered, shocked.

'What do you mean?' Grace said through a strained voice.

'Well, I waited and you never came. I have to admit, I was devastated when you didn't show up, I waited until the last second and when I realised you weren't coming, I was heartbroken.'

'No. no! That's wrong, you never showed up! I was there! I waited for over two hours! I was heartbroken. I couldn't believe that you could do that to me after everything we had gone through. I couldn't return home so ended up going to London. I managed to find a house share and ended up working for an insurance firm as a secretary.' Her voice was almost a squeak as the words came tumbling out.

'Grace, I don't understand, I waited for you, I was there! You were nowhere to be seen, I just thought you'd decided not to go through with it. You knew I could never go back home, I had to go! I was hurt that you couldn't even show up, just to tell me you couldn't go through with it.'

'John, I went to the station as you said, I was there half an hour early, I got there at 4.30 pm!'

'What! I said to meet at 11 am on platform 5!'

'No, you said meet me at 5 pm!'

'No Grace, I didn't,' he spoke softly then. 'Why would I say meet at 5 pm? That would give us no time at all to find anywhere to stay that night.'

Silence fell on them, as they both stared at one another digesting the enormity of what their misunderstanding had caused. Ten long years with both of them thinking that the other one had deserted them when they needed them most.

The waitress broke their silence by bringing their tea over. She hurriedly placed the tea pots and a jug of milk in front of them at great speed, as if she was picking up on the tension in the air between them.

John spoke first. 'I don't know what to say. All these years have gone by now, and I always thought that you didn't love me as much as I thought you did.' He bent his head down staring into his cup as he spoke, avoiding looking directly at Grace.

'Ditto!' she replied, sadly.

Grace sighed. 'Well tell me about your life now, are you married?'

'Yes, I am,' John answered slowly, careful with his words. 'Her name's Margaret. We live not far from here. We don't have any children as yet. I met her at work; she's a secretary at the firm where I work.'

'Tell me about her,' Grace asked.

'Well, she's a few years younger than me; she's really kind and gentle.' His eyes lit up as he spoke about her. 'She's completely different to look at than you; she's as pretty as you are and has blonde hair and is around 5ft 3 inches, and she's quite, well, thicker set than you let's say.' He paused and then added, 'but she's good for me, she keeps me grounded, looks after me and we get on really well. As a matter of fact, we're thinking of starting a family soon,' he said, looking up and smiling.

'That's wonderful news, she sounds lovely. I'm glad you're happy, John, truly.'

'Well, what about you? Are you married?'

Grace held up her ring finger to show off her ring. 'Yes, I am, his name is Peter. Bit of a cliché but I was his secretary too at the firm I was working at. Once we got married, I changed jobs as it seemed a bit strange to be working for your husband,' she laughed.

'Do you have any children?'

'Well strange you should ask, no we don't, but this afternoon Peter and I are meeting with the adoption board.

Peter can't have children, so we are looking to adopt. I'm a bit nervous actually, I've heard they really give you a grilling to check you've got what it takes to become parents.'

'You'll be a marvellous mother, I'm sure you'll both pass with flying colours.'

'I hope so.'

They chatted on for another half an hour with polite conversation, avoiding any talk of the past, then eventually Grace looked at her watch. 'John, I'm really sorry but I'm going to have to go, I'm meeting Peter soon.'

'That's OK, I should be heading off soon. I can't believe what a coincidence it was bumping into each other like this.'

'Yes, in a strange way I feel better now knowing what happened, but I also feel really sad at what could have been,' she said softly.

'Yes, me too... in another lifetime Grace, we'll meet again,' he said, smiling affectionately.

'Yes,' she said. 'In another lifetime.'

They hugged and pecked each other on the cheeks, then Grace left the café and John sat back down looking thoughtful and reflective.

Grace and John had been deeply in love and both had agreed they needed to escape their families. John's father was an abusive alcoholic who would often have fits of violent rages, quite often directed at John. His mother had died when he was young and as the years went by his father got worse. As John got older and stronger, he was finding it increasingly difficult not to beat his father to a pulp. He had to leave the destructive pattern that was starting to take hold of his home life. Grace's parents were part of a religious sect called 'The peculiar people' which preached a puritanical form of Christianity. They were extremely strict and Grace's upbringing was extremely suffocating, leading her to eventually plan her escape with John.

Grace and John were the same age and had met at school. They instantly had a connection, which at first started off as a brother/sister-type of relationship when they were younger, and slowly turned into a deep, intimate love, bound together by their dysfunctional families.

I could see into their futures and knew that they would never meet up again. But this chance meeting had affected them both enormously, as they never quite got over one another, which meant it put a huge crack in their current relationships. They never fully committed to their partners, although both remained married to them until their death. They always held back a little for each other, in case they should ever meet up again. But they never did, only in their dreams and fantasies.

I reflected on how as a human I might have thought a silly miscommunication could not affect a whole lifetime, but I knew that this was part of their life plan, agreed by their souls before they were even born. It was then I saw the beauty of it all, amongst the sadness and heartache, like a perfectly orchestrated series of events. How Grace and John were able to experience a deeper part of themselves and each other by going through this process. Ultimately, they are together within their soul family for an eternity, and they can take as much delicious time as they like experiencing each other from many different aspects, until they can create the highest and the best version of themselves. I move on, willing the next lifetime to come into my awareness.

I find myself in a little garden, full of beautiful roses of all different colours. It's a small garden, but perfectly neat and tidy, as if much love and hard work has gone into it. The grass is a lush emerald green which is completely free of weeds. There is a little pathway of stepping stones leading down to the back of the garden, where there sits a little wooden bench. I can see John sitting there; leaning over with his head bent down, staring at the ground deep in thought. He is smoking a cigarette, which seems strange to me as the John in my lifetime can't stand people smoking. He looks as though he may be in his late thirties. He still has that youthful look but there are little tell-tale signs of fine lines showing around the corner of his eyes. His aura tells me he has the weight of the world on his shoulders. His mood doesn't match the weather, as the glorious sunshine is filling the garden with a beautiful golden light and the sky is of the brightest blue with a few white fluffy clouds gently floating by. I hear the back gate open with a creak and a pair of footsteps make their way around to the back garden.

As John looks up, Grace calls out to him that she is

back. She makes her way over to him. She is dressed in a pretty summer dress, her hair is scraped back in a ponytail and I notice she is wearing make-up, something that I never did in my lifetime. I study her aura and I can see that she has some bad news to tell John. She takes a seat next to him and places her handbag onto her knees. She stares ahead as John turns to her, waiting for her to speak; Grace doesn't look at him.

'Well?' says John. 'What did the doctor say?'

Seconds go by before eventually Grace speaks. 'It's negative!' she pauses while she adjusts herself in the seat then says, 'He said the chances of us falling pregnant now are slim due to my age, but if we feel up to it we should just keep trying naturally. They don't know why we lost the baby and they can't find a reason why I am not conceiving, as everything is fine in both our departments. He said sometimes it's just the way it is.'

They both sit there in silence; the grief of their unborn and unconceived children is obvious. Misery surrounds them both, hanging in the air like a fog. John takes hold of Grace's hand as they continue to sit. Even the beautiful weather cannot lift the sea of despair and pity that tumbles from their bodies. Volumes are being said to one another without a single word being uttered. They are both feeling the pain and rejection of their deepest desires not being fulfilled.

'Do you think that we're just not fit for parenthood and God is punishing us?' Grace said, turning to John.

'I don't know, I just don't know! I look around at some of the scumbag parents there are and think they don't deserve to have their beautiful children. It just seems so unfair. You would make a wonderful mother, you have so much love to give!'

'Don't! Please don't!' Grace shouts, stopping John in his tracks. 'I can't do this anymore! We're just punishing ourselves all the time. Let's just stop trying for the moment. We have each other, we both have good jobs and a lovely home. Let's just take a break from trying and see what happens. There is so much pressure on us. We have our nieces and nephews to love if we need a child fix, I can't wallow in this doom and gloom any longer.' She leans back on the bench looking utterly deflated. The silence that hangs between them is deafening for a while, before John suddenly breaks it.

'OK. Let's just have a break and take stock of things then. Let's enjoy the rest of the summer and go from there,' he said, squeezing her hand. 'I love you Mrs Sullivan, you know that don't you?' he whispered.

'Yes. I love you too Mr Sullivan,' she whispered back.

They sit quietly for some time watching the birds feed off the bird table. As the sunshine intensifies, they both lean back and soak up the glorious rays. Slowly the fog of despair starts to lift as I feel an energy shift start to take place, and I see a pinwheel of light start to appear around them as a spirit comes into view, overshadowing the two of them, encasing them with love of the purest vibration.

It's then that I realise the spirit is James, their unborn baby watching over his parents and coming to give them some much needed love and healing to ease their grief.

As I soak up this precious moment of overwhelming love, I feel their pain and longing for a baby etched in their auras and weaved into their life paths.

I move into their memories and see the beautiful nursery upstairs immaculately set out with a white wicker crib, made up with a pretty lemon blanket set and an array of teddy bears on the dresser. The perfectly hung primrose yellow wallpaper that has little rocking horses and wooden toys dotted about it with curtains to match, waits expectantly. The love and care that has gone into this little room full of possibilities and expectations. The rest of the house is just as neat and tidy as the garden. For a perfectly ordered house, there is an enormous void running throughout, reflecting their unfulfilled dreams, which dominates the whole house. I know that Grace fell pregnant in the spring but lost the baby at ten weeks. Grace and John have been desperately trying for children for over ten years. They were overjoyed when they fell pregnant in the spring and they were so sure that everything would be OK they went ahead early and got the nursery all ready for the new baby. They were both heartbroken when Grace miscarried. They have both had so many tests done to find out what's wrong, and every time they are told that there is nothing wrong with either of them.

Sadly, this was a lifetime where having children is not

meant to be. James and Michael were not incarnated into this lifetime, although they both acted as guides to Grace and John throughout. It was Grace and John's journey to experience their heart-filled desires being unfulfilled. The compassion and love that grew in their evolvement was born out of longing and wanting. In future lifetimes this would stay with them to experience parenthood at a much deeper level.

I leave this lifetime touched by the strength of love that had grown between Grace and John under such difficult circumstances. Knowing that the love of their unborn children James and Michael had still managed to touch them in this lifetime even without them being incarnated.

It was time to move on and I willed another life into my awareness where James and Michael were a part of it. I was finding it easier and easier to manipulate the energies to shift into different dimensions and I was enjoying it. My being was growing and expanding all the time. As I whooshed into the next lifetime, I settled down to watch the show.

I found myself staring back at my reflection in a bathroom that I didn't recognise. Grace must have been in her fifties, as her hair was still dark and I remembered that I used to dye my hair right up until my seventies but I could see the wrinkles and fine lines etched into her face. She was studying herself in the mirror. She was naked from the waist up and I could see her cupping her right breast and manipulating the skin as if she was feeling something inside.

'Are you alright darling?' It was John's voice. She could see him standing outside the bathroom door.

'Yes, I'm coming now,' she replied, quickly getting her brassiere and top back on.

'Only they'll be here soon.'

Grace opened the bathroom door and smiled at John who was standing there clutching a tea towel. He looked just as handsome as ever, but his dark hair was now a distinguished white colour. He was dressed in smart trousers and a shirt. She could hear Christmas songs playing in the background. As they walked into the lounge, she could see a beautifully decorated Christmas tree with lots of wrapped-up parcels underneath.

'I've washed up, what would you like me to do next boss?' he said jokingly.

'I think we're all done darling, shall we have a little drink while we're waiting for them to arrive?'

John smiled. 'Yes what a good idea, what do you want? How about a sherry as it's Christmas?'

'Perfect!'

As John walked into the kitchen to get their drinks, Grace followed him. 'I hope the turkey isn't too dry!' she said, as she opened the oven.

'It won't be, it never is! You always worry too much!'

'I know I can't help it, it's such a responsibility!' she laughed. Just as she put the turkey back in the oven the doorbell rang.

'Oh, that's them,' she cried rushing to get to the front

door. As she opened the door, she was met by a chorus of voices yelling, 'Happy Christmas!'

'Oh, happy Christmas to you too, my darlings! Come in, come in,' she said, leaning in for a hug and a kiss from each of them. Amanda was in first, holding little Mollie. 'Hello, my darlings! Look at you Mollie, all grown up in your new clothes.' She gave her a huge kiss on the cheek then gave Amanda a hug and a kiss. 'What time were they awake this morning?'

'Don't ask! Put it this way, it was still dark!' she replied, pulling a face.

'Oh dear! They'll be tired later!' Grace laughed.

Next in came Jess followed by James. 'Hello nanny, thank you for my present I loved my dolly,' she said flinging her dolly up by the neck for a pretend kiss with Grace.

'You are welcome my precious,' she said, leaning in for a kiss and a squeeze.

'Hello Mum,' said James, breathlessly as he squeezed into the hall carrying a load of bags and various boxes.

'Hello darling, I hear you were awake rather early?' she said smiling at him and giving him a hug.

'Yeah, you could say that! Are Michael and Kate here yet?'

'Not yet but they phoned a little while ago to say they are on their way, should be here any time.'

'Ah that's great, haven't seen them for ages, it'll be good to catch up.'

I could see them all moving forward in a long line,

queueing up for hugs and kisses, first with Grace then with John; it was delightful to watch.

They all took off their coats and shoes and moved into the lounge. Little Mollie went straight over to the tree and started to touch all the presents. 'Nanny, who are these presents for?' said Jess moving over to Mollie and telling her to leave the presents alone, as an older sister does.

'Well, there is a little something for everyone. Father Christmas has dropped some presents off here for you too. But we need to wait until the others arrive.' Grace smiled as she saw the excitement on the girls' faces. Then they were all startled by the doorbell ringing.

'Oh, it's them!' shouted Grace, rushing to the door again like a small child.

She opened the door and there stood Michael and Kate and two little boys.

My heart almost exploded seeing Michael there looking so grown up. He was a man in his early thirties. I only ever got to see him grow until he reached twenty. A huge rush of love filled my being, which saturated the whole house with unconditional love; and to see his wife and children was just the most beautiful thing. I knew Kate, she was his girlfriend in my life. She was very pretty, a petite 5ft 2 inches compared to Michael's 6ft 1 inch frame. She had dark blonde hair and big china blue eyes but she looked so different now, she seemed so mature. This was something that I used to dream about when the boys were growing up. How privileged I felt watching this loving family occasion unfold in front of me.

'Hello Ma!' said Michael.

'Hello darling, it's lovely to see you, how are you all? Up early?' Grace asked smiling.

'Yep! We sure were!' replied Michael, making his way into the hall.

I continued to watch, glued to what I was seeing. I couldn't get over how grown up Michael and Kate looked, I couldn't believe they were both parents. Standing beside them were two gorgeous-looking boys. One looked about nine years old and was the spitting image of his father, he had the same dark hair and olive complexion. I discovered his name was Tom. The other little boy looked a couple of years younger and looked just like Kate, he had the fairer hair and complexion although his eyes were brown like Michael's. His name was Sam. They looked adorable. My beautiful unborn grandchildren.

For the rest of the day, I watch my wonderful family have a lovely day of festivities. Watching them eat Christmas dinner around the table, listening to their general chit-chat and banter. The children got on wonderfully, playing with each other's games all afternoon. I noticed how their auras shone brightly and their energies filled the entire house. I stayed around them and got as close as I could sending my love out to all of them, feeling joyous at what futures lay ahead for all of them in this life.

Although Grace would go on to discover that she had breast cancer, it was caught early and after treatment it *would go into remission allowing her to live out the rest of her life without any other health concerns. John was able to retire early as he had amassed financial freedom to do so, allowing them time to travel the world and enjoy their grandchildren. James would re-train to become a counsellor and would go on to open up a very successful practice. Michael would work in the environmental field where he would specialise in the eco-energy field, something that suited him perfectly. This was a good life for all of them, one where they all thrived as a family unit and, apart from Grace's cancer scare, they didn't really have any major traumas.*

I thought it couldn't really get much better than this and savoured this life into my being before journeying on to other lifetimes. I carried on weaving my way through the veil into different dimensions witnessing all the different lifetimes I have lived. As I did so I felt my soul swelling as layer upon layer was joining it. I could feel the depth and experiences of my lives consolidating as each life was added to the pot. Knowing that my higher-self was connected to these lives all along. In my lifetime as Grace Sullivan, I could have connected to the knowledge and the wisdom of all of these lives through my higher-self. A whole library of books at my disposal, now I knew what Oto meant when he said that we didn't need anyone else to answer our questions, if we go within it is all there ready and waiting to help, we just need to connect.

I felt as if I had grown from a tiny acorn to a giant oak

tree by the time I had visited all of my lifetimes and past lives. As I came out of the fog, I could see Eli coming in to view. Beside him was Oto. They were both waiting for me with open arms. I stepped forward and merged with both their energies. I felt the unconditional love flood through my being and radiate out into the Akasha. A powerful union of beings, creating a dazzling display of a blinding white light with bright sparks of colour exploding out into the cosmos. I noticed my energies were far more powerful now and were nearly matching Eli and Oto in strength. I had one more step to go before I would complete this lifetime. It was time for my own life review.

Chapter 10

Life Review

'It is time,' Oto said. 'The elders are waiting for you.'
   I feel the presence of Oto and Eli beside me and feel ready to take the next step. I gesture my readiness and we start to move together in unison, out of the mist and through the crystal door. We find ourselves back out in the brilliant white corridor from where we originated. Oto leads on, guiding us through more winding corridors, as Eli stays by my side blending with my energies as we move along; offering me little ripples of comfort along the way.

   Eventually we find ourselves standing outside an ornately decorated pair of giant doors, made out of what looks like mother of pearl. They have carved into their centre, two beautifully crafted angels with their wings spread out. As I look closer, I can see different crystals embedded all over the doors; all offering different vibrations, gently shimmering and vibrating. As we make our way through them, we find ourselves in a huge blue room with no walls, floors or ceilings. At first, the blue looks as if it's the sky, but then I realise it's the palest blue energy, vibrating at a very high level. Ahead of us is a long table with a row of beings in human form seated behind it; in front of the table is a large circular platform with a domed roof covering it. The dome is see-through and looks to be made of glass, but on further investigation I realise it is fluid and discover it's actually made of water. The feel of the room is exhilarating. As soon as we enter the room, our beings expand instinctively as they soak up the pure energy surrounding us. I am beckoned to move closer and feel awestruck as I take in the panel of beings in front of me. At the centre of the panel, leading the review, is a beautiful lady, her hair is dark with tinges of red and is flowing down to her feet. She has olive skin and chocolate-brown eyes. She is wearing a simple white robe as a backdrop to her breathtaking beauty. A shimmering aura of gold is radiating around her being. Her face is full of love and kindness and as she speaks, using telepathy, her smooth soft velvety voice fills my being with love and compassion.

'Greetings Asa, beloved one, love and light to you blessed one. We are so pleased to see you return.' As she speaks, the energy in the room increases and I feel a tidal wave of pleasure surging throughout my being. As her energy hits my very core, I instantly know this lady to be Mary Magdalene; I have always had an inexplicable connection to her in my current lifetime, and I know now that we have been connected in past lives. I know the Bible's story of Mary Magdalene to be false, she was a very important part of the spiritual movement. Jesus and Mary were both born onto the Earth 12 days apart. Mary was born first followed by Jesus, the alpha and the omega; for without one the other was not complete. They were like the positive and the negative of a battery, needing both to function. They were incarnated together to raise the vibrations of mankind and show us the way. There is no male or female in the spirit world, but on the Earth realm both sexes were needed to restore the equilibrium and exist in the duality. It was fear that led man to turn their back on Mary and condemn her to the shadows. The power of the female essence with her nurturing qualities and strength of endurance scared certain men and led them to feel impotent and powerless, causing leaders of this time to bury the female goddess deep underground and to remain hidden for many years to come. However, as we know now, just because we can't see something doesn't mean it does not exist or it is not powerful. In recent years on Earth, the female essence has been emerging from the shadows and balance is being restored. For where we have man we have woman, both of equal value but differing in their strengths and abilities and this is now being recognised and celebrated.'

I move closer towards her. 'Thank you beloved one, it is good to be home.' Mary's presence is foremost in my feelings but I feel across the rest of the panel to take in the other elders. I immediately feel the presence of Jesus to the right side of Mary. He is wearing a simple white robe too, *he has a thick growth of facial hair covering his face and shoulder length hair which isn't quite as dark as Mary's, and his skin is not as olive. His eyes are mesmerising, they are so dark but soft and kind. His aura is powerful, almost blinding and you can see the energies between the two of them almost blended together as one. To the left of Mary is the apostle Paul, he has a strong green energy emitting from his being. Again, he is dressed simply in a white robe, his hair is very dark and curly, but not as long as Jesus'. His energy is radiating out love towards me. The three of them are a formidable force, it is difficult for me to make a connection with the other elders.*

As I feel this, Oto connects with me and explains that the reason I am feeling the energies with Mary, Jesus and Paul stronger than the others is because I have a connection with them in a past life. Another person may have different elders on their panel as it's important that the person having the life review has a connection with them to feel safe and loved. I am grateful for this, I could not think of any other beings I would rather have on my panel than these beings in front of me. The unconditional love I feel for them is overwhelming, it is a total all-encompassing feeling of the purest love and joy.

I move forward to blend with their energies, and feel my being catapulted into a higher level of awareness vibrating at a level of pure love. I instantly connect with the lifetime that I spent with them and feel like I have slipped back into an old pair of shoes, feeling comfortable and familiar in their presence once more.

'We have been watching you Asa in this lifetime, and feel great joy that your soul's life plan has been followed, and you were able to experience and understand love in this lifetime at the highest level.' She paused, and we continued to soak up one another's energies. 'Blessed one, your soul family is here to watch your life review. Are you ready to commence?' she said softly.

As she says this the familiar whooshing feeling overcomes me as I feel a collective energy swoop in all around me. I feel John (whose name I now know as Era), Michael, my mother, my father and my sister's energies, championing me on as if they are my number one fans. There are no words spoken, only an all-consuming and yet tender love that surrounds me, raising my vibrations to a higher peak. Outside of my close family, I feel the rest of my soul family draw close and sparks of gold start to bounce off our auras as the room turns a beautiful blue and green.

Eventually it is time for me to stand within the clear dome. I make my way through the water that looks like glass and float above the platform. Surrounding me are the most glorious beings of love and pure joy, all willing me to do well and raise my evolvement to a higher level from this lifetime.

Mary stands up in front of me. 'Are you ready, beloved one?'

I gesture that I am.

'Then let us begin.' She raises her hands and the water

starts to turn from clear glass to a torrent of waterfalls cascading all around me. I feel my being stretch out from my very centre to the farthest edges of my aura, then feel myself implode, scattering into millions of different moments all around the dome. Everything happening at once, I am watching scenes of my life like they are from a movie. I can see and feel the moment of my birth. The pain I feel entering down into the birth canal, being squashed and taken away from the comforting safety of the womb. The fear I experience being born as the cold sensation hits my skin, and the noise from the outside world reverberates all around me. I can feel my mother's pain, but also the relief when she sees me for the first time. The overwhelming love that rushes into me from her energy field. How safe and loved I feel as she cuddles and caresses me, hearing her gentle cooing noises as she rains soft kisses all over my head and face. I feel the love of my father as he sees me for the very first time, holding me with tears in his eyes; being so gentle and tender with me; as well as the love he feels for my mother as she gives him the most precious gift a man could have.

When I am introduced to my older sister, I feel her uncertainty towards me as she examines me, as well as her jealousy and insecurity in the early days of my arrival. I feel this from the other perspective too, as I feel the same uncertainty and jealousy when my younger sister is brought home. Every thought, action or deed that I ever have is radiated out to the wider collective, like a pebble being thrown into water as the ripples stream out. Every smile that I give, or act of kindness that I make, is felt a thousand-fold out into the greater circle.

As well as my own feelings, I also feel what other people are experiencing too. My being is expanding out, gloriously rising up to a higher level of existence. It is then I feel for the first time little feelings of hurt that start to invade this loveliness. Starting with tussles over toys or struggling to share with my siblings as a toddler, to the more painful feelings of name-calling at school.

I am brought to a memory of being at primary school. There is a boy in my class who is a quiet, studious child who happens to have very thick, bushy eyebrows. There I am with my best friend Rachel making up a horrible little rhyme about his eyebrows. How clever I think I am and how we laugh at the poor boy's expense. As I witness the boy's reaction to this, I can see his aura shrinking and a darkness start to descend around him from my energies. A sharp pain slashes across my energy field like a razor blade as I feel the feelings this boy is enduring from my cruel actions. I then feel the pain intensify as the feelings spread out further to the boy's mother. Her feelings of hurt at her son's pain and her anger directed at me. This then ripples out even further as it spreads to the father's pain, the grandparent's pain, the wider family's pain. All increasing the pain and discomfort I can feel throughout my being. Shame washes over me to an unbearable degree until I feel my soul family surround the dome and send in healing vibrations that filter into my being to make it more bearable. Even though these are the actions of a silly schoolgirl, they are still callous actions and cause the poor boy a lot of pain. What is so shocking are the powerful feelings I inflict on the other family members as well. They feel such a strength of love for the boy that when they see him so upset, it causes huge pain for them too. I am touched by the beautiful connection of love and kinship that exists so deeply within, that when one is hurt, the rest of the family hurt. It is in that moment of pain and hurt that I am overwhelmed with the realisation of what pure love truly feels like. Such adoration and tenderness radiating out an all-consuming devotion to one another of unconditional love.

Which brings me to another significant moment in my lifetime. Again, it is in my childhood when I am about six years old. I have asked a younger little girl up the road to come and play with me. We are playing teachers. I am the teacher, of course, because I am older. The younger girl is very timid and shy; she struggles to give eye contact and hides behind her glasses. The energies she emits gives her a sense of being a bit of a victim. As I am playing with the girl, I can feel myself getting bossier and bossier. The growing feeling of power feels good. I am a middle child and always have an older sister to boss me around so I am enjoying feeling this moment of power. As the power starts to grow in my energy field, I find myself shouting at her to put her hand up before she speaks. So, the little girl nervously complies. But instead of allowing her to speak, I leave her with her hand up in the air, watching her squirm in pain and enjoying her discomfort, relishing the feeling of power and control. Eventually the little girl starts to cry so I let her put her hand down but only because I think I might get into trouble.

The next day I call for her again, looking forward to playing the same game, only this time I am met by a furious mother who tells me never to call for her daughter again and practically slams the door in my face. It is at this point that I feel totally ashamed of myself and very remorseful. This is totally out of character for me but I enjoyed the feeling it gave me and now I can see it for what it was, an act of cruelty and bullying. I never see the girl again from this day on but the feelings of shame and remorse stay with me for the rest of my life. Whenever I feel the flames of desire for power come into my being, I instantly think of the moment I was met with a mother's wrath and the cold waters of shame and remorse extinguish the flames. I discover that the mother and the little girl are from my soul family. Our brief contact serves a lesson for me in this life in how to overcome the dark side of power and control and I am never seduced by it again.

Another lesson that shines through to me is that given by my teacher. There was a very quiet girl in our class who was completely overlooked by the rest of us. She used to merge into the background at every opportunity. She wasn't bullied or anything like that but it was as if she was invisible. Nobody noticed her; she was very good at keeping *out of the way. One day, as the teacher was handing out our writing books, she started to sing to the girl, very softly but it was with total adoration of the girl. It was only for a few moments but it had a profound effect on the class. As she sang, the girl suddenly came alive, it was as if she was being coloured in and brought into everyone's awareness. Like a light had been shined upon her and we suddenly had a new member of the class arrive. I can still remember looking at the girl like it was for the very first time. She was actually a pretty girl with beautiful dark, brown eyes and very long eyelashes. After that moment, things changed for the girl. She started to get invited to birthday parties or included in conversations. She started to shine, not in a boastful way, but in a beautiful way as if life had been breathed into her by a few moments of absolute undivided attention given to her by the teacher in a very loving and nurturing way. In those few seconds of song from the teacher, I experienced the feelings of awakening radiating from the girl in a very powerful way. It was a wonderful feeling of aliveness, of acknowledgement, of being present. In my years following this moment, I have always looked for the invisible people, the wallflowers, and made a point of showing them I can see them with a few words of kindness. Wonderful energies from all of those moments flood into me, raising me higher in exhilaration and gratitude as the feelings I evoke in others are sent back to me ten-fold. What a wonderful teacher she was and how simple acts of kindness can enrich so many lives around us.*

As I move on, I feel sadness wash over me as I remember the confusion I felt when my father went away to the war. It seemed to happen so quickly. There was lots of talk of the war but I wasn't sure what that meant. I feel my mother's fear gripping her as she is crying and clinging on to my father. I do not understand what is about to happen. My father's fear is strong as well. I can feel he is more worried for our safety than that of his own; another example of unconditional love which floods throughout my being.

Then I feel pain and emotional damage escalate as it rampages around the adults in the wider family, as loved ones are drafted up and sent off to fight. My fear of not knowing but sensing something is wrong in the adults overwhelms me, and I feel protectiveness towards my younger sister who is distraught at her daddy disappearing and her mummy not being emotionally available to her. Even at this young age I feel that I mustn't burden my parents with my wants and needs and I try to help bridge the emotional gap that has developed between my mother and us, by helping to placate my sister and burying my fears.

Several months after my father went away, we were told that we were going on a little holiday to the countryside and were going to stay on a farm. We didn't realise that our mother was not going. Suddenly my sisters and I find ourselves on the station platform boarding a train saying a tearful farewell to our mother. I can feel my *older sister holding on to her strength, trying to be brave for us, and how I tried to stay brave too, but I was terrified. Luckily, we were evacuated to a lovely farm in Wales, to a childless couple who owned a dairy farm. How they loved us all like their own. I could feel the love radiating from them, encasing all three of us, keeping us safe and loving us like their own for four and a half years. My younger sister didn't even remember our parents, she considered our foster parents as her real parents. At first, we cried for our parents often, but with the gentle love and tenderness shown to us by our foster parents, after a year or so we stopped asking or talking about them. How we loved those years on the farm, surrounded by the animals. My older sister's love of horses meant that she was able to ride out every day over the fields checking on the cattle. We all had such freedom, all of our free time was spent outside running wild, swimming in rivers, rolling down hills. We never really felt the effects of the war. Sometimes we would see planes fly over and hear adults talk about the war, but it was a very small community and we were sheltered from all of the horrors. I can feel nothing but pure love shining through me in this period of my life, even though I was separated from my parents. It shows what extraordinary people our foster parents were. However, as my thoughts turn to my parents, I can feel longing and pain radiating from my mother. Her difficult decision not to visit us, worried that we may become unsettled, and her anguish at being parted from us stayed with her throughout the war. She was tormented at making that decision by trying to convince herself it was a brave thing to do, as it was paramount that we stay alive and keep away from the destruction of war. When I think of my father, I feel the absolute terror he experiences going into battle; the filth, hunger and deprivation he endures at war; watching men die in agony in front of him. The uncertainty of whether today would be his last day. Grieving for the life he had, never knowing if he would ever have normality again in his lifetime. All of these thoughts and feelings came flooding into my awareness. Emotions upon emotions sweeping over me in waves, bringing clarity and awareness.*

When the war ended, I see our foster parents sitting us down at the kitchen table, telling us that we were going to be going home to our real parents. How my younger sister screamed at the mention of leaving them, as our real parents had become a distant memory to her. The overwhelming sadness and shock that we all experienced knowing this was all going to come to an end. How torn I was, wishing to stay in this blissful existence but also feeling loyal to my real parents, as although my memories of them were dim there was a huge part of me that still felt very connected to them.

I now know that my foster parents wrote to my real parents asking if they could keep us. But this was met with a firm no. However, there is no bitterness from either side. I feel the love and gratitude my real parents felt towards my foster parents shining through. There is no anger at the decision they made, only huge sorrow and pain from both parties that descends throughout my being. We never saw my foster parents again after the war. I visited many years later when I was a mother with my own family but sadly they had both died, childless and having never adopted or fostered again after us. I can feel the warm feeling and memories that I had on my visit to the farm flooding through me, grateful for the love that they gave us. Such a sacrifice my parents made out of love and duty. I feel my parents love surround me as well as my foster parents; a united front of warmth and love reaching out to my being. Knowing these spirits are my kin and have loved me over many lifetimes, I settle into the comfort of their love.

As moments move on, I experience the highs and lows that life has to offer. My life choices mean I am blessed with a lot more highs than lows, which means that my being experiences the magnificent highs of stretching out with waves of pleasure and sheer ecstatic joy, oscillating throughout my energy field. The lessons that I learn from any lows I feel, which are at times painful, are in themselves a success. I need to experience these lows, these mistakes, to enrich the life that I lived. They are as important as the highs and celebrated as such with my soul family.

There are many other little incidents where members of my soul family very briefly enter my life to help with different teachings. Most of the time the meetings are felt as hostile, or I dislike the person intensely as I feel they have it in for me. How differently I can see things now. I feel the *love of my soul family around me once more as I soak up the love and healing energies radiating out towards me.*

As my life unfolds in front of me, I am able to feel every single moment and every impact that I create in the universe with my thoughts, actions and deeds. Most of my feelings are that of pure joy, love and euphoria at the life I have lived. The love that I feel for my family and friends. The ecstasy I feel at meeting John, how well matched we are, both sharing so many passed lives together. I can see how our past lives have impacted this current life, how the depth of our relationship is made on solid foundations built up over many lifetimes. How blessed I am to experience the richness of this love. As I reach my meeting with John, a huge tsunami crashes around my being, full of excitement, ecstasy, longing and desire. As I savour our wedding, my being stretches out to immense proportions. The rush of elation and sheer joy and happiness vibrates throughout my being, leaving me floating on a sea of breathtaking, exquisite, unconditional love, which also radiates out to my soul family in vast magnitudes. So many happy, loving moments we share together, experiencing our boys growing up, feeling so complete and whole in my role as a mother. I was born to be a mother in this lifetime and I adored it and treasured it.

When I reach the moments of the birth of our children, my vibrations amplify to euphoric proportions. There are no words to describe the surging love that blasts throughout my energy field. My soul expands out, thriving in a blissful state of consciousness. I feel my energies blending with my children, merging together as one. I know this to be true as I feel the impact of Michael's departure from Earth. As his silver chord is cut when he leaves this dimension, I physically feel the pain in my heart of his untethered soul leaving my energy. Although essences of his being stay within my energy field for the rest of my life, the pain of his leaving is torturous. I try to keep the lid shut to Pandora's Box that resides within me, holding in my deepest and darkest moments of grief. As the memory of the police arriving at our house reaches my awareness, the steel box violently opens sending an explosion of catastrophic proportions out into the atmosphere. A howling vibration comes crashing out like a force of thunder hurtling to the outside of the dome. A pain rips across my energy field tearing me into pieces, scattering me out in all directions. I feel my being twisting and turning all over the place as confusion and torment oscillate throughout my energy field. As the power of this eruption reaches its climax, I feel my kin expand to reach out and catch it as the force rips into my soul family and they absorb the explosion, like a huge mound of cotton wool smothering a giant bomb.

The fierce power of my soul family's unconditional love for me rears up and extinguishes my darkest bouts of grief which have been locked up and left unattended for far too long, leaving it to turn to a disturbingly violent energy.

When Michael died it felt like a huge chunk of my heart had left with him, leaving me feeling hollow and *empty. My whole inner world had exploded out like a bomb going off, leaving me feeling shell-shocked and numb for many years. Unsure for the next few years whether I would ever have the ability to truly love again. The darkness of my energies over the next few years are evident. The pain of Michael's departure also sends a tsunami of waves hurtling out to the wider family as I feel the pain felt by John and James and the wider family and friends.*

As I acknowledge these emotions, pure love of the highest vibration filters into the dome, soothing and restoring my energy fields. I feel pieces of me start to conglomerate into larger pieces, until eventually the beautiful unconditional love sent to me on waves of vibrations with the most glorious sounds, restores me to the perfect being that I now know I am.

As with earlier when I feel the love evident through the hurt and pain of the family of the young boy, I also feel the overwhelming love evident as it shines through the grief and the pain. I become aware of Michael's life plan and my agreement to play my part in it. As the bigger picture emerges into my awareness, light floods into my being as my soul starts to swell and flourish at the momentous choices and actions that I have made following Michael's departure. The pain and the suffering start to lift and dissipate as the light floods through my being, raising me to a higher vibration. As I start to rise, I can feel my whole soul family around me rising simultaneously too, to a higher state of being.

I become aware of all the crossovers from other lives led as Grace Sullivan. All the déjà vu moments that occur. The adjustments I have made to this life because of things I have experienced in my other lives as Grace Sullivan. All teaching me lessons in how to understand and experience love.

Finally, I come to the end of this lifetime. My last glimpse of this life is watching James sleeping as I transition into heaven.

I discover my soul's purpose in this life is to experience love through loss. To experience love by strengthening my relationships to my kin. To raise my vibration through acts of love and kindness and in turn help raise the vibration of the planet. I am one of the light workers that Oto has talked about. The same as my god-daughter Ann. Oto knew this but left me to discover this for myself. So many wonderful emotions are filtering into my being; the pride and joy of raising my vibration to such a high level in one lifetime. The awareness that this is a collective victory, that needs my soul family to play a part in my life as I have in theirs, whether it is incarnating together or remaining in heaven to act as a guide. We all selflessly play a part for the greater good of evolvement to reach the higher divine energies of 'All That Is'.

As the waterfall around me starts to calm, I feel my presence coming back into the blue room. As the water settles and turns back to what looks like glass again, I can feel Mary's presence in front of me. I also feel Eli step forward to stand by my side.

'Beloved one, your journey in this lifetime is now at a crossroads. You must choose whether you want to remain in heaven or whether you want to return to Earth to continue this lifetime.'

I feel my soul family draw even closer to me. The thought of returning to the Earth into my old decrepit body was not an appealing one at all. How could anyone choose to go back after experiencing such wonderful energies in this magical place called heaven? Then I think of James and Amanda and all my brood of grandchildren and great-grandchildren. Then I know that for some, the love of their family left behind would be a strong pull to go back. However, if I was to return I know that my life would split off and carry on running in another direction parallel to my old life, still continuing without me. So I know my family would still feel the pain of my departure. I feel I have accomplished what I set out to do in this lifetime. I have said my goodbyes and would only serve to be a burden to them. It's James's turn to become head of the family and lead them down the middle path. I am incredibly proud of my son and I know he will rise to the role in hand. There is no time in heaven so I know I can flit backwards and forwards, up and down and in and out of Earth's time to see my beloved family. So, my decision is an easy one to make.

'I choose to remain in heaven.' As I make my decision, my being expands out to merge with my soul family's *energies.*

Mary bows her head towards Eli and he bows back at Mary, bringing his hands together in a prayer pose in a respectful manner. He then moves away from my side.

'Very well, blessed one. I now call upon Archangel Michael to cut the silver chord.'

Suddenly there is an almighty thunder of energy, as Archangel Michael swoops into the blue room. His energy is huge, dwarfing our energies around him. A beautiful golden yellow and orange is surrounding him as he unfolds his wings and reaches out with his sword made of clear quartz and sugilite crystal. I can feel him reach for my silver chord and tug it as he raises his sword and slashes across it to sever the connection.

As he does so, a lightness immediately washes over me. I feel as if I am diluting into the Akasha around me. My being starts to vibrate at a faster and higher frequency. My awareness expands out and merges into my soul family where every tiny detail of every life, moment, thought, deed, and action of the whole of my soul family is evident. I now have access to a much bigger master plan where everything is perfectly orchestrated. A beautiful symphony of life is playing out all around me. Every time I think I have reached a greater understanding of love and what it truly feels like, it is blown out of the water as I move up the ladder of evolvement to the higher realms. I am experiencing senses that I didn't even know existed. The senses of the human experience seems so basic compared to the extraordinary experience I am having in this moment. No longer am I in human form. Everyone now shows themselves in their natural state in spirit form and I truly feel as if I have come home, welcomed into the loving heart of my family.

Chapter 11

The Collective

W̶e drift into a new existence after the melding has taken place, there is no 'I' any more as the 'I' is now part of the collective that is our soul family, feeling everything as a whole. We have left the blue room and are now residing in the beautiful energies of 'All That Is'. The powerful vibration of 'AUM' is oscillating throughout our collective being, sending shivering delights of ecstasy rippling out into the universe. Healing is taking place as a group as we have now increased our vibration and moved up the ladder of evolvement. We are bathing in sheer joy and love at being reunited once more. Increasing our colour and vibrancy and once more returning to the natural state of our being.

In the collective we are one in the only ocean of being that there is 'All That Is'. Flowing in the timeless sea of perfection in pure ecstatic joy. So different from the life in the illusion of separation.

Life in the separate is spent exploring and experiencing the different rivers of life that flow. At times you will enter the river in the calm, and start off with a less challenging life, only to exit in the chaos of the choppy rapids. Other times you may enter in the chaos of the rapids, only to master these and exit in the quiet stillness of the calming waters. But regardless of where you start and where you finish, what is clear is each separate identity will experience the same river over and over again until every twist and turn is discovered and experienced. Over many lifetimes the separate will build up knowledge of the same river, whether in the calms or in the rapids. And in turn will build up knowledge and understanding, mastering creation and manifestation to ease the path of the separate one. After each river is mastered, the separate will move on to another river to explore with another identity.

Being together in the collective is our natural state where we can heal and recoup after such an arduous journey of experiencing the illusion of separation. Enjoying the everlasting cycle of raising and deepening our vibrations through the process of evolution; allowing us to reap the rewards together by floating in the purest, highest energies of 'All That Is.'

At some point, an awareness starts to descend over our soul family for a need to split off. Now the healing has taken place, essences of Michael (Ata), John (Era) and Grace (Asa) split off and return to the part of their beings from the life they have just led. They find themselves back at the lake. They are now waiting for James. Although they know he still has many Earth years to live, they happily await his return, for in heaven there is no time. They will have the pleasure of witnessing his life from the realms of the Divine. Acting as a guide and watching over their lovely Earth family.

They now spend existence together, floating in and around the glorious lake, resting on the porch at night to look up at the stars shining in the sky like diamonds. John has taken them to his heaven too, a beautiful desert island with stunning clear azure waters surrounding it filled with beautifully coloured fishes of all shapes and sizes. John always did like the ocean. He leads them to fly over the water then dive down amongst the magical dolphins. As they swim amongst them, they communicate with the dolphins, as in heaven you are connected to every living thing. Even the grass and the trees and the water are living beings that they are able to connect and communicate with. They are overjoyed to spend this existence together in such a peaceful, harmonious way, blissfully happy at being at one again, moving in and out of each other's heaven.

As they continue in this state of consciousness, they choose once more to divide their essences up again into three parts. Part of their essences will stay here continuing with this blissful existence in their created heavens and part of their essences choose to remain close to the Earth realm around James and his family, offering love and assistance in any way that they can.

The third part of their essences take on roles in heaven. Michael is working with newly transitioned spirits that have been born into heaven after committing suicide. Part of his life plan in his last life was to experience poor mental health and eventually death by suicide so he can have a deeper understanding of the turmoil that ensues with newly returned souls, following suicide.

Many poor souls need a higher level of help after transitioning following suicide as they feel a huge amount of guilt at the damage caused to their family. Michael said that seeing Grace moving on with her life and still being able to give and receive love following his suicide, helped him enormously in his life review, as it eased his suffering and pain and he was eternally grateful that Grace was able to do that. The suicide rate is increasing drastically due to shifts being made on Earth. Many people are feeling unbalanced and out of kilter with the shifts of energies happening at this time. Society may seem as if it's in chaos at the moment but changes are being made for the better and the Earth is raising its vibration and so is the collective. Balance will be restored and big changes will have been made to the way our governments work and the way we treat the planet. Michael now has the tools and experience in his being to be able to help at a much deeper level.

John is working with newly created spirits. When 'All That Is' releases another droplet from its vast ocean of consciousness, a new spirit is birthed. The soul is then created and then formed into a collective to make a soul family. Every soul family is unique and will have different numbers in the family. Sometimes there can be hundreds or sometimes thousands within a soul family. The soul family lives out their lives over and over again until they can finally reach the higher realms of the Divine to once again merge back into 'All That Is', making way for another droplet to be released once more, to start the journey over and over again for all of eternity. When a new soul family is created, extra love and support is given to guide them on their journey, just like parents of a newborn baby will do. They will spend time in heaven adjusting and growing, spending time in school, although not the type of school they have on Earth. With John's patience and compassion, he is perfect to assist with the teaching and learning for these new spirits.

Grace is now assisting Sia with healing work in the halls of healing. She is connecting with healers on Earth acting as their guide and she is also training fellow spirits in the art of healing. She has been healing in-between lifetimes and is now a teacher to others. She is connecting with other humans in meditations too, some of them are part of our soul family. Grace's great-granddaughter will show an interest in healing when she comes of age and Grace will act as her main guide to help her develop her gifts. On the Earth plain more people will turn to holistic healing and avoid prescribed medications with nasty side effects. Doctors will start to work more with holistic healers and many surgeries will have a holistic healer attached to it as standard. Scientists and the medical profession will start to become interested in energy healing and see the benefits of it in all areas. It will become the norm to have energy healing before and after operations to assist with recovery. Society will value their mental health more and start to make the links that their emotional well-being is synonymous with their physical health. There will come a big shift when people will value their time and their health more than they value their income. We will come out of the shallow material world and start to become more creative and at one with the beauty and nature around us.

Our soul family now vibrates on a very high frequency, what a beautiful journey we have all faced together. So much love in the collective, valuing the challenges we have been through as much as the rewards we have received. Knowing that there is only perfection among us, for there is no other possibility, for all that exists is 'All That Is'.

Chapter 12

The End of the Beginning

As the sun filters into the room waking James from his sleep, it slowly starts to dawn on him that his mother is no longer a part of this world. It has been nearly twenty-four hours since he got the phone call from the care home to say that his mother has died peacefully in the night. Even though he knew it was coming, he was still devastated at her passing. He can't shake off this horrible feeling of being so alone in the world now. He knows he still has Amanda and the kids but he feels like an orphan at the grand old age of 61. He feels too ridiculous to tell anyone, after all his mum was well into her eighties and has lived a long life with good health. He feels lucky that his mum has lived so long, some people lose their mothers at a young age. Nevertheless, he feels strange and abandoned. When his dad died, he still had his mum. He was still surrounded by his dad's things at the bungalow. It just felt like Dad was on a long holiday and had sort of morphed into one with Mum. But now they had both gone, it was like grieving for Dad as well as Mum. It was the end of an era, no more would he be visiting his family home, with all the usual furniture, ornaments and photos dotted around the place. Even his link to Michael had gone now. He lay there taking everything in, and slowly trying to plan a timetable of the day ahead of him. He had to go over to the care home sometime today. They were keen for him to collect his mother's things so that the next poor soul could move into her room. At some point he had to go and visit his mother in the chapel of rest. He also had to start thinking about planning the funeral. He felt sick, anxiety swept over his body and he could lie there no longer.

He gently crept out of bed, as Amanda was still asleep and he didn't want to wake her. He put on his dressing gown and went downstairs and made himself a cup of tea. He then sat down in the armchair in the lounge which looks out into the back garden. It was a beautiful spring day already. The sun was shining and the dew on the grass was sparkling like diamonds, it looked so pretty. Mum would have loved this, he thought. He sat quietly for some time, just staring out into the garden, deep in thought, silently sipping his cup of tea. He noticed a little robin had flown down and was taking some food from the bird feeder. He watched it flitting about pecking at the mealworm, then flying down onto the patio to eat it. The robin slowly moved closer to the window until it started to stare in at him. It unnerved him slightly. He was still feeling unsettled from the morning before. He had dreamed about his mother, he could feel her presence strongly and as he was awakened by the sun streaming through the window, he opened his eyes and thought he saw his mother floating at the end of his bed, only to disappear in a flash when he blinked. He didn't think much of it at first, as he knew his mother was on his mind a lot anyway, he just thought his mind was playing tricks. It wasn't until he got the phone call half an hour later to say that she had died that he became a bit unsettled. He didn't really believe in the afterlife but he knew his mum did. He so wanted to believe but it seemed too far-fetched. He felt it was more than likely people's minds playing tricks on them because they so wanted it to be real. Now here he was staring at a robin, who most definitely appeared to be staring back at him. His mum had threatened him with sending a sign to him once she had passed, but this couldn't be a sign, surely? No. It was just a robin being curious. It's still early and the robin probably wasn't expecting an audience, so it's come to investigate, after all they are supposed to be quite friendly birds.

Eventually the robin flew away, back to its little bush in the garden and James got up to make some breakfast. He could hear Amanda upstairs moving around, so he put the kettle back on to make her some tea.

'Morning,' Amanda said groggily, as she came into the kitchen yawning. 'You're up early, did you struggle to sleep?' she said, as she gently draped her arms around James in a comforting embrace.

'Yeah, I did, I just had so much going through my mind I couldn't lay there any longer.' James nestled into her neck for a moment, then moved away to finish making the tea. 'I'm going to head over to the care home this morning and collect Mum's things, then I thought I might go to the chapel of rest to see Mum.'

'Sure, that sounds a good idea, do you want some company?' she asked softly.

'No that's OK, I'll go by myself today, then we'll go again to see Mum together and see if any of the kids want to go. I just feel I want to do this alone today if you don't mind?'

'Of course I don't darling, whatever you want to do is fine by me. I just don't want you to think you have to do this alone. We're a team, right?'

James smiled. 'Yeah we are, and a good team at that,' he said, turning and giving her another hug.

After breakfast, James went up to get ready, then after phoning the care home to check it was OK for him to go over, he headed out the door. He reached the car door and unlocked it ready to step in when he remembered he hadn't got his phone. He quickly dashed back up the path and opened the front door calling out he'd forgotten his phone. He was waiting for Amanda to do a false laugh at him, which is something over the years they did to one another. It was childish really, but it was their thing, falsely pretending to laugh out loud at one another if they forgot anything and had to come back. But today was different, Amanda just called out not to worry and to take care driving. His heart did a little flip at the gesture she had made and in that moment he knew that he loved her just a little bit more than before, if that was possible.

He headed back out and walked towards the car. As he did so he thought he saw something flitting about in the car. It must be a leaf or something blown in through the open door he thought. As he stepped into the car and sat down, he was faced with a little robin perched on top of his steering wheel. He sat there frozen to the spot, hardly daring to breathe. The robin stared back at him and there they sat for what must have been about a minute. Slowly, he reached his index finger out to the bird only to see it jump on to it, using it like a little perch. They continued to stare at one another; emotion started to overcome James as his eyes became glassy and a large single tear started to fall from his eye.

'Well, I'll be blown,' he whispered. Slowly a huge smile crept upon his face. 'You were right all along, Mum.' Somehow, he knew that everything would be alright, as now he knew for certain that this wasn't the end.

Printed in Great Britain
by Amazon